MURDER AT ST. PAUL'S CATHEDRAL

A 1920S COZY HISTORICAL MYSTERY

A GINGER GOLD MYSTERY
BOOK TWENTY-FOUR

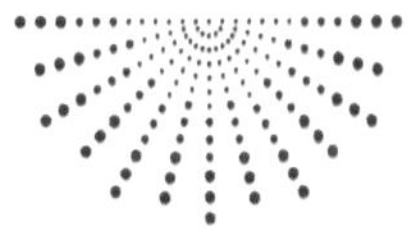

LEE STRAUSS

Murder at St. Paul's Cathedral

Copyright © 2023 by Lee Strauss

Cover by Steven Novak, Illustrations by Tasia Strauss. All rights reserved. No part of this book may be reproduced in any form or by any electronic or mechanical means, including information storage and retrieval systems, without written permission from the author, except for the use of brief quotations in a book review.

Library and Archives Canada Cataloguing in Publication

Title: Murder at St. Paul's Cathedral / Lee Strauss.

Names: Strauss, Lee (Novelist), author.

Series: Strauss, Lee (Novelist). Ginger Gold mystery ; 24.

Description: Series statement: A Ginger Gold mystery ; 24 | "A 1920s cozy historical mystery."

Identifiers: Canadiana (print) 20230451691 | Canadiana (ebook) 20230451705 | ISBN 9781774092699 (hardcover) | ISBN 9781774092682 (softcover) | ISBN 9781774092712 (IngramSpark softcover) | ISBN 9781774092705 (EPUB) | ISBN 9781774092675 (Kindle) | ISBN: 978-1-77409-412-9 | ISBN: 978-1-77409-413-6 (D2D) | ISBN: 978-1-77409-503-4 (bookvault)

Classification: LCC PS8637.T739 M865 2023 | DDC C813/.6—dc23

CHAPTER ONE

"They don't make Agatha Christie write under a male pseudonym."

Ginger Reed, known by some Londoners as Lady Gold, considered her former sister-in-law Felicia's words. Since her marriage to the Earl of Witt, Felicia had been known in high society as Lady Davenport-Witt, a title she wore well. Gifted with a pretty, heart-shaped face and fashionable rosebud lips, Felicia had learned how to put her charm and beauty to work. Thankfully, she'd outgrown her single contemporaries' wild yet lazy ways and had stepped into a sophistication that suited her new status.

"Mrs. Christie's latest book was quite good," Ginger said after a sip of tea. Boss, Ginger's loyal Boston terrier, was curled up on the lemon-yellow settee with Ginger in the Hartigan House sitting room. She scrubbed his ears. "Have you read it?"

Felicia sniffed. *"The Mystery of the Blue Train?* I'm in the middle of it now. Oh, Ginger!"

Ginger stared back at Felicia in alarm. "Is something wrong? Are you in pain?"

"I'm in pain of heart! I fear I will forever be known in the literary world as Frank Gold!"

Ginger admired Felicia's successful foray into the world of mystery fiction, and her propensity for drama and melodrama suited the venture. "Would you rather be known as Lady Davenport-Witt? Or Felicia something or other?"

"I suppose Lady Felicia Davenport-Witt would be rather ostentatious." Felicia waved long fingers—nails nicely done in bright crab-apple red, Ginger noted—through the air. "Oh, bother. I don't think I want to write anymore, anyway."

Ginger blinked back in astonishment. "Why not? You're not going to let another writer's success push you out of the running, are you?"

"No, it's just that, to be honest, Ginger, I feel like my creativity has dried up." Felicia wrinkled her dainty nose. "Not just a bit. I haven't written anything of worth for weeks. Seriously, months."

Ginger gazed at Felicia over the rim of her teacup

as she postponed responding by taking a sip. Her tactic worked as Felicia continued, unprompted.

"It's not like they pay me that well, nor do I need the money. So, I asked myself, what would I rather do with my time?"

Ginger pushed a lock of her red, bobbed hair behind one ear as she fought back a grin. "And what did 'yourself' say?"

Felicia narrowed her eyes in response to Ginger's jesting tone. "*Myself* said, 'Take photographs!'"

"You do have a lovely camera," Ginger said.

"You're thinking about my Voigtländer Bergheil. Though I love its impressive accordion-style face, it still uses plates, which are only optimal for studio photography. I've picked up a handy Kodak Brownie for my new job at the magazine. It uses film!"

"Film is more convenient," Ginger admitted.

"I do enjoy snapping photographs," Felicia added, "and Charles got a man in to build me a darkroom."

"I also have a darkroom here," Ginger said. She ran a private investigative business that required plenty of photographs to be taken, though not of the creative type. Mostly the kind that caught people doing things they ought not to be doing. "There's also one at Lady Gold Investigations."

Felicia wrinkled her nose. "I don't think Magna

would appreciate me using the space there for my own pleasure. Besides, she scares me a little."

Ginger chuckled. Magna Jones was a brilliant and efficient assistant, but one would never refer to her as sweet. "She scares me a little too."

"I plan to take a lot of photographs, so it will be best if I have my own darkroom," Felicia said, "but thanks for the offer."

"Any time."

"And . . ." Felicia leaned in conspiratorially. "I already have an assignment."

"An assignment?"

"I'm contracting myself out as a freelance photographer for *The Sketch* magazine. I know I don't have much experience, but I showed a collection of my photographs to the editor, and he liked them enough to take me on."

Ginger was intrigued. "What's the assignment?"

"I'm snapping photographs at a wedding." Felicia's grey eyes sparkled. "Not just any wedding. The Duke of Worthington's wedding at St. Paul's Cathedral. I was surprised he was allowed to get married there, but then I learned he had obtained a special licence from the Archbishop of Canterbury."

Ginger's throat went dry. She'd met the current Duke of Worthington before, when she'd investigated the deaths of the former duke and his wife.

There was much talk about the nuptials of this duke, formerly known as Lord Percy Heath, and his much younger bride-to-be. She choked out, "Is that so?"

"Are you all right, Ginger?" Felicia inclined her head. "You look rather, um, stricken."

"I'm fine. My foot's falling asleep." Ginger made a show of uncurling her legs and stretching them out in front of her. She gazed blankly out the window, as her mind worked on the problem newly presented. Felicia didn't know that her grandmother, the dowager Lady Gold, had been keeping a decades-long secret that could turn Felicia's world upside down if she should learn of it.

But how could attending the duke's wedding reveal the truth? There was no real danger in that, was there? Except the anonymous note that had arrived a few weeks earlier, dismissed by Felicia but not forgotten by Ginger.

Dearest Lady Davenport-Witt,

Your name was GOLDen, but what is its real WORTH?

The truth is stranger than fiction. Do you want to know it?

I do.

However, no new missives had arrived for Felicia, at least none that she had mentioned.

Ginger crossed her ankles casually as she spoke. "I'm sure it will be an exciting experience and you will produce photographs that will please your editor."

"I hope so."

"You know, I just recalled a memory of another time we had tea together in this room. You'd received a strange note. Do you remember it?"

Felicia cocked her head. "It's funny you should bring that up."

Ginger held the dread she felt in her gut, keeping her expression blank. "Why? Have you received another?"

"I did—just last week. A nuisance note was written by someone with too much time on their hands. I'm afraid I've thrown it into the rubbish bin."

"What did it say?"

Felicia's thinly plucked eyebrows arched high as she looked upwards, remembering. "It started the same as the other one, addressing me by my married name, and then something about the wedding of the year and how everyone who's anyone would be there." Her eyes latched on to Ginger. "It was what gave me the idea to approach the magazine." She lifted her chin and added defiantly. "Believe it or not, Charles and I weren't invited."

"And now, through the magazine, *you* are," Ginger said.

"That's right!" Felicia crossed her legs at the knee and bounced her stylish shoe, a broad-strapped suede-and-leather pump with daring two-inch heels. "It's brilliant, isn't it, Ginger?"

"Indeed," Ginger said with feigned enthusiasm.

"Wait." Felicia's jumping leg stilled. "Were you and Basil invited?"

Ginger's husband was a chief inspector at Scotland Yard, and occasionally she and he would work a case together. "Yes, but we likely made the guest list because we had a previous connection with the duke," Ginger explained.

"Right." Felicia shivered. "You and Basil solved the murders of the late Duke and Duchess of Worthington."

Ginger nodded.

"Is Grandmama going too?"

"She wasn't invited either."

"Ooooh, that must've got her goat." Felicia laughed. "Grandmama doesn't like to be excluded."

Ginger didn't think Ambrosia minded this time around. The elderly matriarch had nearly insisted that Ginger and Basil decline their invitation.

Ginger had soothed her by saying it was better for someone to attend to observe and report back, just in case. In case of what, Ginger didn't know, but Ambrosia had been mollified.

"She'll just have to read about it in the papers," Ginger said, smiling benignly at Felicia. "Look at all the wonderful photographs you're sure to take."

"I suppose that'll have to do for Charles, as well," Felicia said with a pout.

"You know," Ginger started, "I bet I could get you and Charles an official invitation if you'd like."

Felicia's eyes lit up. "That would be splendid. It would be nice to share the experience with my husband. At least some of it."

Ginger nodded with understanding. Charles was a busy man. She wondered if he realised he was becoming guilty of neglecting his wife.

CHAPTER TWO

Felicia breezed through the front door of her Mallowan Court home. Even though she could be living in a grander residence in Belgravia, she felt that this house—Witt House—was more manageable and to her liking. Besides, she loved living across the cul-de-sac from Ginger. Though they were no longer sisters-in-law, Ginger was one of Felicia's best friends. No. Her *very* best friend.

Since marrying Charles, Felicia's connection with London's bright young things had waned. Her friends complained that she'd become uppity and "frightfully serious". Felicia had gone out with them early in her marriage since Charles spent a lot of time away from home, but she felt that sort of behaviour—the drinking, smoking, and flirting into the wee hours of the morning—didn't suit her new station in life. She loved Charles and didn't want to do anything that would put him in a bad light, even if done in complete innocence. Charles was highly esteemed by his peers and could've had his pick of any eligible lady in Britain, or the world for that matter, and he had chosen her. She was honoured and delighted. Thinking about Charles deepened her longing for him, and learning from their butler, Burton, that she'd just missed his telephone call was like a dagger of disappointment.

"Oh no!" she lamented in response.

"I'm afraid so, madam," Burton returned. Felicia had only recently learned that Burton had been Charles' batman—a soldier assigned to serve an officer—during the Great War. That explained the bond between the men and Burton's unwavering loyalty. It also explained the bulldog protectiveness of his master he'd exhibited when Felicia had entered the picture. Now, she better understood why he hadn't trusted her, but thankfully, all that suspicion was now water under the bridge.

Burton held out a silver salver containing a stack of sealed envelopes. "Perhaps there's news in the post that will brighten your day."

Felicia scooped up the post with a grateful smile. She and Burton had started off on the wrong foot, but things were going swimmingly between them now.

"Thank you, Burton." Felicia started towards the sitting room as she flicked through the envelopes, glancing at the return addresses. Oh, one from the picture editor at *The Sketch*!

She hurried to the sitting room where a writing desk was kept and was about to reach for the letter opener when a smaller envelope fell from the pile, landing on the Axminster carpet. Swooping to pick up the errant envelope, she became aware of a dismal sense of recognition.

Really! Whoever this person was needed another hobby.

The typewritten card inside read:

Dearest Lady Davenport-Witt,

Does one know who one is? Do you know who you are?

The truth sets one free. Or does it cheat, steal, and imprison?

Felicia almost threw the note into the bin, then remembered that if another note arrived, Ginger wanted to see it. She planned to walk the letter over but completely forgot about the errand after opening the post from *The Sketch* editor.

Dear Lady Davenport-Witt,

Please forgive the short notice, but I thought you would be interested to know that the Duke of Worthington and his fiancée will be dining with friends at the Ritz tonight. The news has only recently come to us.

Felicia hummed. Someone had leaked the couple's itinerary. She read on:

If you would like to take photographs upon their arrival, I suggest you be in front of the hotel by seven.

Felicia flicked her wrist and stared at her time-piece. Nearly five! Dropping everything else on the desk, she rang the bell for her maid, then ran up the stairs to the bedroom she shared with Charles. "Daphne!" she shouted.

Her maid appeared with a look of consternation on her face. "Madam? Is everything all right?"

"Everything is terrific. I need help getting ready to go out." She waved for Daphne to follow her into the bedroom. "Time is of the essence!"

CHAPTER THREE

Felicia had an enviable wardrobe, nearly as impressive as Ginger's, but having so much choice was nearly as difficult as having too little, as one could become frozen with indecision. If it hadn't been for Daphne's intuitiveness, Felicia might still be standing like a statue, staring blankly at all the hanging fabric.

As it was, she now donned a sensible two-piece summer suit, suitable for the pleasant June weather. She'd worn exquisite gowns to many opera and high-society events, but this was not one of those, at least not one where she was a guest. Felicia wondered briefly why that was so but shook off the interfering thought. She was on her way to the Ritz in a professional capacity! Wearing her leather driving gloves, she drove her *car*—she considered the term "motor car" to be outdated—to the prestigious hotel with far less honking guiding her way than Ginger could boast.

Ten years earlier, one could count the number of motor cars—cars—on the streets of London with one hand. Now it was difficult to find a lowly horse hauling its owner's wares about the city. Traffic lights had been installed at major intersections, and overworked police officers managed the other junctions with hand signals and a strong whistle.

A crowd had already gathered at the entrance of the Ritz, and for a dark second, Felicia feared she'd missed the arrival of the couple *du jour*. Scrambling to park her Mercedes-Benz, Felicia caught the kerb with one white-rimmed, spoked tyre, a move reminiscent of Ginger. Grabbing the strap of her camera bag, she locked her car door and then pushed her way through the small mob.

"Press," she shouted. "Please make way!"

Her qualifications were a bit of a stretch, but she was there on behalf of a magazine. They'd even given her a badge. "Press!"

After a few uncomfortable elbows to the ribs, Felicia pushed her way to the front. "Have they arrived?" she asked the perturbed-looking man beside her. He wore a trench coat and a trilby and was busy scribbling something in an opened notepad, barely giving her the time of day.

"Not yet, sweetheart. Toffs have a different sense of timeliness to us common folk."

Felicia flashed the man a sharp look, her mouth gaping open. First, she wasn't his sweetheart; second, she found the term "Toff" belittling. As one, she was quite capable of showing up at an event on time. Even if she often didn't.

Someone shouted, "There they are!"

As if it were one creature, the crowd turned.

Another shouted. "Miss Wright, are you excited about your wedding?"

Felicia nearly scoffed aloud. What a silly sort of question. Of course Hazel Wright was excited. What bride wouldn't be?

But she wasn't there to ask questions or to take notes. Felicia prepared her Kodak Brownie. She clicked the button once the bride-to-be and the groom were in the frame. The duke looked handsome in his waistcoat and tie. Indeed, he was older than most grooms, closing in on his seventies, but he had a suave essence about him. One would say debonair. He tucked his fiancée's hand through his arm, protecting her from the boisterous crowd.

Miss Wright, a bright young thing, was a sight to behold, looking like the duchess she was soon to become. Felicia was pleased, having situated herself in such a good position. She continued to snap photographs until the couple had disappeared inside.

The doorman remained on the steps. "Show's over, folks." He waved an arm, shooing them away. "You'll have to wait until the wedding."

Not for one moment did Felicia consider that the man was referring to her. As the others moved away, she headed up the stairs. The uniformed employee held out a palm. "Not today, madam."

"But I'm Lady Davenport-Witt," Felicia said with all the indignation she felt. "Are you *really* going to prevent me from entering?"

The doorman gave her the once-over, and Felicia was suddenly aware of her simple suit and sensible shoes.

"You're a lady, eh? Then why are you dressed like one of that lot, taking photographs for money?"

"I . . . it's something to do. Look, mister, I don't have to answer to you!" Felicia fished around for her handbag. Wouldn't the man be ashamed when she presented her identification! She was married to an earl, a member of the House of Lords, for heaven's sake! To be denied access to the Ritz Hotel in this manner was unthinkable. He'd thank her to keep his job.

Felicia's hand made several swipes over her suit

jacket, coming up empty, and she suffered the sickening realisation that she'd left her handbag in her car.

"Madam," the doorman started kindly. "Perhaps you can come again another time." A subtle nod of his chin told Felicia he was asking her to return when she was properly dressed, his eyes round with a silent plea that she not make a scene.

"Very well," she said. As a lady, it wouldn't do to cause a disturbance. "I shall return shortly." She pierced the security guard with a steely glare. "You shall remember me when I return, I assure you."

CHAPTER FOUR

*G*inger was more than happy to join Felicia on a "reconnaissance mission" to spy on the couple at the Ritz. Felicia had returned from her photography shoot in a sour mood. It wasn't the first time Ginger had seen Felicia work herself into a tizzy, but it had been a while since something had set her off.

Ginger thought the time spent getting ready—Felicia was lucky that Ginger was the sort of person who could change plans at the drop of a hat—would work to cool Felicia down, but she was still in a temper as she drove the two of them back to the Ritz.

"Can you believe that?" Felicia said with indignation as they approached the front entrance of the prestigious hotel. "There's been a change of doorman!"

Ginger had had an ear full on the way there, and Felicia had been looking forward to confronting the doorman who'd offended her and was planning on rubbing his social misstep in his face.

"That isn't the same man?" Ginger asked.

Felicia huffed, confirming. "Blast him."

"Well, you've certainly dressed the part now," Ginger said. The two of them had dressed in becoming cocktail gowns with unsymmetrical lines and shimmering sequins, which were all the rage in the summer 1928 fashion catalogues. Ginger had chosen a beaded silver skull cap with dangling bits that shimmered in the light, whilst Felicia had donned a complementary turban.

The security guard gave a welcoming nod, and the doorman smiled. "Welcome to the Ritz hotel, ladies."

The luxury hotel would take a newcomer's breath away. The marble floors glistened, reflecting the light of the grand chandeliers that hung from high above, themselves a masterful work of crystal and gold plating. The walls were covered in lush paper with fanciful designs. The spacious lobby held plush, modern chairs and exotic plants in large clay pots.

Fresh flower arrangements were strategically placed, adding sophistication and a pleasant aroma.

A gilded sign propped up by the doors to the cocktail lounge informed guests that a private affair was happening behind the varnished doors. A porter stood to one side, his white-gloved hands cupped at his belt.

Felicia stared at Ginger. "We have to get in."

"Why?" Ginger asked. Despite being desperately curious, keeping Felicia out of the duke's life seemed more prudent. "The restaurant is lovely. We could have a glass of wine." At Felicia's withering look, Ginger added, "Or something stronger."

"You've been acting strangely lately," Felicia said with a note of accusation. "The Ginger I know would be conspiring with me, curious to see the old duke and his infant bride."

"Perhaps I'm maturing," Ginger said. "If rather late in life. You don't have to follow in my footsteps in that regard."

"Ginger!"

Ginger huffed half-heartedly. "Very well." She approached the youthful-looking doorman and batted her eyelashes. "Good evening. I'm Lady Gold and this is Lady Davenport-Witt. We seem to have forgotten our invitations."

The doorman's gaze moved from Ginger to

Felicia and back, flashing with a look of uncertainty. Ginger counted on the British class system to work its magic, and eventually, turning away two ladies proved too much.

"Of course, my lady," he said, then opened the door to let them in.

Fortunately, a couple of empty chairs were available, perhaps left by a couple who hadn't been able to make it at the last minute, and Ginger guided Felicia to them.

"Look at them," Felicia whispered rather loudly, and Ginger gave her a warning look. Felicia lowered her voice further. "Have you ever seen such a mismatched coupling?"

As the words left Felicia's mouth, the duke, his white hair oiled back off his forehead, draped an arm around the young lady's thin shoulders. She turned to him with bright eyes, staring with unabashed admiration.

"As the saying goes," Ginger returned, "beauty is in the eye of the beholder."

"There's certainly nothing wrong with *his* eyes," Felicia said. "Do you think their love is real? Or do they have some business agreement and are just putting on a show?"

"It's hard to say," Ginger returned. She was

wondering the same thing. And if so, what kind of deal was it? "I suppose that's between them."

Typically, Ginger wouldn't even give it a second thought, as what went on between other couples was none of her business, but Felicia had a stake in this instance. If only she hadn't promised Ambrosia that she wouldn't talk about Felicia's bloodline!

"Who's that?" Felicia nodded discreetly to a table near the front occupied by a lady wearing a flowing lavender gown. Her eyes were narrowed and calculating. "She doesn't look happy for the couple."

Ginger had to agree. "I recognise her. That's Lady Eliza Banks. I wonder if she fancies the duke as well."

"He's an eligible bachelor," Felicia said. "Lady Eliza appears to be closer in age to him and might've been a better fit. But men like the younger ones."

"Some men," Ginger amended.

"I'm going to visit the ladies," Felicia announced. "I need to powder my nose."

Ginger answered Felicia's implied question. "I'm in no need."

Felicia gave a short nod before grasping her small, stylish handbag, and walking away. Ginger was glad to have her gone for a few minutes, giving her time to approach the bride and groom.

With a broad smile, Ginger held out her gloved

hand to the duke. "Congratulations, Your Grace." The Duke of Worthington did a double take and accepted her hand. "Mrs. Reed?"

"You do remember me," Ginger said lightly. "I wondered if you would."

A shadow of darkness crossed the duke's face. "I could hardly forget the circumstances under which we met."

Miss Wright, her eyes darting in question, reached for her groom's arm. "Darling?"

"Oh yes, please forgive me," the duke said. "This is Mrs. Reed. We met on the sad occasion of my brother- and sister-in-law's deaths."

Miss Wright stared back at Ginger with distinct suspicion. "Is that so? I don't recall seeing your name on the invitation list, Mrs. Reed."

Ginger blinked at the bride's brashness.

The duke also seemed rather taken aback by the lack of polite propriety. "Hazel!"

"Do forgive us, Mrs. Reed," the duke said. "This wedding, though joyous, has been rather stressful at times as well."

"There's no need to apologise," Ginger said amiably. "I understand bridal nerves. I won't keep you, Your Grace, Miss Wright. I just wanted to congratulate you in person whilst I had the chance."

As Ginger returned to her table, her mind

worked on the nuances of the interaction that had just played out. Miss Wright, despite her childlike demeanour, was clearly intelligent and calculating. Her affection for the duke was like that for an old uncle. Percy Heath could possibly claim romantic passion, but Hazel Wright wasn't in it for love. The question was, what was she in it for? Money and title, to be sure, but was there more to it than that?

"Ginger!" Felicia had returned to their table, her fingers drumming on the top in agitation. "Why didn't you wait for me before moving in on the duke and his bride-to-be?"

Ginger flicked a hand before taking her seat. "People have been milling about them this whole time, and then they were suddenly alone. I just took advantage of the opportunity."

Felicia narrowed her eyes, then exhaled as if she'd decided to accept Ginger's explanation. "Well, what did you learn?"

"Not a lot. They both seem a bit fatigued, to be honest. As if the events leading up to the nuptials have been unpleasant."

"When they arrived, the duke helped Miss Wright out of the car, looking as proud as a peacock, but she seemed less than pleased as she stepped out."

"Interesting," Ginger murmured. However, now that she'd seen the engaged couple and spoken to them, she felt the whole affair underwhelming. "I'm ready to leave whenever you are, Felicia."

But Felicia was focused on something, or rather someone, on the other side of the room. Following her gaze, Ginger's breath hitched when she saw the object of Felicia's attention.

"Doesn't that waiter look like Charles?" Felicia said.

The man certainly looked like the Earl of Witt to Ginger. She sat across from Felicia and had a different viewing angle. She made a show of squinting. The man who looked like Charles caught her eye before quickly disappearing behind a large areca palm. "It's not him," Ginger said, believing she'd just told a fib. "Just a man who looks like him."

"You mean to say Charles has a doppelgänger?"

Ginger smiled as she gathered her handbag. "Don't we all? Now, I am feeling a need to go home. I'm afraid I've hardly had a moment for little Rosa all day."

CHAPTER FIVE

The following day, Ginger enjoyed breakfast with Basil in the morning room of Hartigan House, where the French windows offered a lovely view of the flower beds in the back garden. Basil's position as a chief inspector at Scotland Yard provided him with a flexible work schedule, depending on the busyness of the criminal element in the city. When Ginger had first met Basil on the SS *Rosa* on the journey across the Atlantic, he'd only been a handsome fellow passenger who'd caught her eye, but it was his police work that had brought them together. Their romance had been fraught with challenges, and the fact that they'd faced them and overcome them made their relationship all the stronger.

Ginger watched her husband as he sipped his

morning tea and felt a warmth of admiration. Basil only seemed to grow more handsome with time. His hazel eyes were bright and tender, at least when he was considering her. The wrinkles that fanned from them only seemed to enhance their attractiveness, and the growing silver in his temples made Ginger want to run her fingers through his hair.

She didn't, of course, but the desire for her husband was certainly there. Unfortunately, the time and place weren't suitable for expressing emotion.

Basil caught her eye as he stared at her over the rim of his teacup. "What are you thinking about, love?" He placed his teacup on its matching saucer and grinned. "I can see your wheels turning."

"Can you believe it has been five years nearly since I moved back to London?" At the time, Ginger had thought she would sell her childhood home and return to America. Fate had had other plans! Not only did she not sell, she'd since remarried, adopted a son, and given birth to a daughter. She'd established herself as a lady in business after opening a successful Regent Street dress shop and a private investigations office. She'd become reacquainted with her late husband's family—his grandmother, the dowager Lady Gold, and his sister Felicia—both of whom had moved in with her shortly after she had decided to stay in London. Felicia had also married and moved with her new husband across the street from Hartigan House. This situation greatly pleased Ginger, as she counted Felicia as one of her dearest friends.

"Time flies when you're having fun," Basil returned. He kissed her forehead and whispered, "And I'm having the time of my life."

"The feeling is mutual, Chief Inspector," Ginger said cheekily.

"By the way," Basil said, his mood sobering. "I imagine you've been following the news of the Duke of Worthington."

"Yes, in fact, Felicia nearly dragged me to the Ritz to crash a pre-wedding celebration." Ginger proceeded to fill Basil in on the experience.

"Looks like things are finally going the gentle-man's way," Basil said.

"It certainly seems like it," Ginger agreed. "After so many years as a bachelor, one can't help but wonder what caused him to take the plunge into matrimony so late in life."

"It's probably nothing more than the old fellow is lonely," Basil said. "Or more to the point, wants to produce an heir to the title."

Ginger frowned. "She's young enough to be his granddaughter. However, that's hardly my concern.

Miss Wright will be a wealthy woman when nature takes its course."

"This sort of transaction between a man and a woman is as old as time," Basil said. He inclined his head knowingly. "It's not always the lady who benefits financially."

"Touché," Ginger said. Because of her vow to the Crown, she couldn't share everything about her past with Basil, but she shared all the parts that she could, including her first marriage. It had started as an arrangement—the Gold title for Hartigan money—but ended up as true love.

"I'm concerned about Felicia." Ginger pushed her plate away and refilled her teacup. She wished she could share that Charles, in disguise, had also been at the pre-wedding event and had clearly not expected to see Ginger or his wife there. It raised the question: why was the secret service interested in the Duke of Worthington, and particularly, why bother to infiltrate an event leading up to the nuptials?

"Oh?" Basil said, his brow raised. "Is she in one of her moods again?"

Felicia was renowned for being quick to feel strong emotions, whether joy, anger, or anything in between. "No," Ginger said, "nothing like that. She's been receiving nuisance notes."

Basil's hazel eyes flashed with concern. "Threats?"

"Not to her life, but . . . more about exposing her secret."

"Secret? What secret?"

"Well," Ginger hedged. "It's more Ambrosia's secret. Felicia is unaware of certain facts, so the notes don't make sense to her."

"But they make sense to you," Basil said, leaning back, "because you know Ambrosia's secret."

"That's correct."

"I see. And you find yourself in the predicament of having to reveal Ambrosia's secret to protect Felicia."

"That's also correct."

Basil took Ginger's hand and squeezed. "I think Ambrosia would want you to protect Felicia. I can't help you if I don't know the threat. Do you have the notes?"

"Just the last one."

"How many are there?"

"Only three, but Felicia threw one away."

"Three is three too many."

"I can tell you the gist of the notes. The writer hints boldly at something that involves both Felicia and the Duke of Worthington."

Basil gaped. "I didn't see that connection coming. Do tell."

Ginger glanced at the door, ensuring no one was about to enter, then with great reluctance uttered softly, "The duke is Felicia's great uncle. Ambrosia had a dalliance with the duke's brother when she was young. She was already expecting Felicia's father, Robert, when she married Artemis Gold."

Basil exhaled sharply. "Well, bowl me over with a feather. Does Charles know?"

Ginger shook her head, though the truth was, she didn't really know what Charles knew.

FELICIA ENTERED the morning room of Witt House to find Charles already seated for breakfast. He was as pleasant as usual, standing to welcome her to the new day with a gentle kiss. He quickly returned to whatever newspaper story he'd been reading, his dark brown eyes moving down the columns. Beyond him, out the window, the flower beds were blooming.

Without glancing up, Charles muttered, "You're staring."

"Am I?" Felicia said noncommittally. She took a careful sip of her tea. "What news story of the day has so captured your attention."

Charles chuckled and folded the newspaper, laying it down. "You don't like to share me with anyone or anything, do you, my love?" He reached for her hand and brought it to his lips.

Felicia's heart softened. She'd been so worked up about what she thought she'd seen—her husband at the Duke of Worthington and Miss Wright's pre-wedding event—that she'd had herself convinced he'd been lying about his true whereabouts when, after cornering him the evening before, he'd insisted he'd been at his club having a few drinks with friends.

"No, I don't," Felicia returned with a note of petulance. "I'm overcome with jealousy most days and rather despise the House of Lords for taking you from me so often."

Charles' eyes darkened at the outburst. "Consider it your duty to the Crown," he said simply. "All the ladies of the lords must endure it."

"I'm not so sure about that," Felicia said stubbornly. "I ran into Lady Birtwhistle not long ago, and she said Lord Birtwhistle spent rather a lot of time at their manor, only attending a few times a year. I got the impression she wouldn't have minded in the least if he spent more time away."

"Lord Birtwhistle is elderly," Charles said gently,

then smiled. "I'll be sure to become bothersome to you when I'm his age."

Felicia pouted. "I want you to become bothersome to me now."

Burton, who'd stepped into the breakfast room so quietly Felicia hadn't even noticed he was there, cleared his throat just as Charles retook her hand. If Felicia hadn't known better, she'd have thought the butler was jealous. Charles pulled his hand away and turned. "Yes, Burton? Is there something you need to tell me?"

"No, sir. My apologies. Just something caught in my throat. Shall I bring more coffee?"

"Very well, Burton. Thank you."

Burton bowed and left the room.

Charles turned back to Felicia. "Why don't you book a getaway for us for the end of the month? I should be finished with my current responsibilities by then, at least for a couple of weeks."

Felicia wondered why they always had to "get away" to be together, but she would take what she could get. "Where shall we go?"

Charles wiped his mouth with a linen napkin before placing it on his dirty plate, and then, as if considering, stared out the window. "Wales," he said. "It's lovely this time of year."

Felicia pushed down feelings of suspicion. He'd

suggested Scotland the last time they'd had a similar discussion, and he still found reason to be busy with work.

"Why don't I surprise you?" Felicia said, watching Charles for his reaction. If she hadn't known him as well as she did, she would've missed the slight tick of his right eye, the only giveaway to his displeasure at her request. Her heart tightened. *Why does this bother Charles? And why doesn't he admit it does?*

Charles' smile came a second too late to be believed by her. "Of course," he said. "That would be delightful. Let me know as soon as you've chosen, as my curiosity is certainly piqued." He stood, leaning over to kiss Felicia on the cheek.

Felicia raised her chin and tilted her head to make the task easier. "Back to work?"

"I'm afraid so," Charles said. "Try not to stew, love. Spend your time planning our next holiday."

Felicia didn't comment either way, as she planned to do both. Choose a holiday destination whilst stewing over why her husband refused to be completely honest with her. He was entangled with something complicated and clearly thought she wasn't fit to know, or worse, that she didn't have the intellect to comprehend.

With a huff, Felicia pushed away from the table. Suddenly her diary for the day became clear. A visit to her travel agent was in order. If only there were time for a jungle tour in Africa or some other place far from England. That would likely be the only way she'd ever get her husband's body and soul to herself. Perhaps whilst lying together in a primitive tent far away from the House of Lords and the trappings of London, Charles would cast off whatever demons bound him and finally be honest with her.

Because one thing was clear: it most definitely had been Charles at the Duke of Worthington's dinner. What did the two men have to do with each other? And why would Charles lie?

Percival Heath, the Duke of Worthington, and Miss Hazel Wright's wedding day arrived the next week with a blustery wind. Ginger readied herself in her bedroom, the very room she'd lived in as a child but had since decorated to suit a married couple. The wooden furniture was large and ornate against walls painted green and trimmed with white. Gold-and-white-striped chairs sat beside the long windows, a table between them.

Lizzie, Ginger's maid, was helping her dress for the occasion, buttoning her champagne-coloured gown that was covered with a sheath of gold netting. Three-tiered layers of the skirt were trimmed with large embroidered roses. Matching embellishments topped the shoulders. "This wind, so strong it's stirring up dust and debris, it's not a good omen, madam," Lizzie said, fastening the last button on the back.

"Indeed," Ginger returned. "Not that I believe in superstition. But the bride might, poor dear." She added the last bit to ensure she sounded sympathetic, but due to her brief encounter with Miss Hazel Wright, Ginger didn't believe the lady to be of fragile sentimentalities—she was slyer and more fox-like. Instead of wistful romantic fantasies that could be crushed by poor weather, Miss Wright was probably champing at the bit to get the ceremony over with, making the nuptials legal. How soon, Ginger wondered, before the duke's health waned?

Ginger shook her head. Best not to let such morbid thoughts enter her mind. Such things resulted from years of encountering humanity's worst hearts and minds—through the war years and since.

"Hopefully the wind will settle before the festivities."

"It's such a grand event." Lizzie's pixie face gleamed as she placed a crystal-encrusted headpiece on Ginger's head. "It's all anyone is talking about." She sighed. "Miss Hazel Wright is so beautiful. You must be so excited to be attending."

Excited wasn't the first word that entered Ginger's mind. "It's sure to be a memorable event."

Ginger spent time putting on her make-up, then posed in front of the floor-length mirror in the corner of her bedroom, opposite her dressing table.

"You look lovely, madam," Lizzie said. "Oh, I almost forgot. Lady Gold has asked to see you in the drawing room before you leave."

"The drawing room?" Ginger's preparation had been delayed by Rosa, who'd been fussy with a new tooth. Basil, Felicia, and Charles were waiting in the sitting room. That Ambrosia had chosen the drawing room was telling.

"Yes, madam, the drawing room," Lizzie confirmed.

Ginger made her way down the curved staircase, letting her gloved hand slide gently along the broad wooden banister. Being mid-morning, the grand chandelier above was unlit. Ginger's mind flashed back to when her father had had it installed. Everyone was so excited. The male servants bustled about providing the tall ladders and bracing them as the men who were installing the light carefully lifted it over their heads. The female servants were all present, too, watching with bated breath. Ginger, a small child then, watched the spectacle from a hiding spot behind the large potted palms at the entrance. She recalled hearing the housekeeper say, "Dear Lord, I hope they don't drop it. What a disaster it would be to clean up all that glass."

Thankfully, the new light fixture had been installed without a hitch. Originally, there were candles that Pippins had to light—a task he didn't relish as he didn't like heights. Their faithful butler did his duty, regardless. However, when electricity came to Hartigan House and was ultimately wired to the chandelier, Pippins could hardly keep a hint of a smile from his naturally stoic expression.

Reaching the black-and-white-tiled floor of the entranceway, Ginger could hear muffled voices from the sitting room—the tenor sounds of Basil and Charles and Felicia's playful giggle. Ginger wished she could join their joviality, but she had to attend to Ambrosia first.

The dowager sat in the drawing room—a vast area with modern velvet furniture in the shade of jade situated in a semicircle around the large brick fireplace in one corner, with a grand piano in the other, and enough floor space to host a dance. Ambrosia occupied her favourite chair, the lone leather wingback, her posture unnaturally straight and stiff because of the unfashionable corset she insisted on wearing. Her grey hair had grown longer and was in a neat bun at the back of her neck, her maid Langley's handiwork. Ambrosia had succumbed to social pressure a while back and had had it cut short, an event she referred to as an unfortunate lapse of sound judgement.

Ambrosia's hands—blue veins prominent under translucent skin—were clasped on her lap. Ginger's former grandmother-in-law loved her jewellery, even when she wasn't planning visitors or an outing: large rings were displayed on large-knuckled fingers, and a large diamond-framed brooch featuring a cameo of Queen Victoria was pinned to the collar at her throat. She stared with large round eyes when Ginger walked in.

"Good day, Grandmother," Ginger said. "You wanted to see me?"

Without returning a greeting, Ambrosia got right to the point. "You know I didn't want you to attend this wedding. And you're dragging Felicia too!"

Ginger bristled. She wasn't dragging anyone. "Consider that our absence might bring more attention to our family than our presence. This is the social event of the year. Those in our social class would be singled out for not attending." With a look, she added, "We can excuse one family member, but not all."

Ambrosia frowned, the map of wrinkles on her face deepening. The dowager Lady Gold didn't like being bested. "Please promise me you'll keep Felicia from him."

Ginger studied Ambrosia with compassion. A secret of this magnitude must've been a heavy burden to carry for her long life. Ginger could only imagine how Ambrosia trembled inwardly at the threat of being exposed after all this time. It would be an unkindness, and a troubling way to come to the end of one's life.

"I'll do my best," Ginger said. "With the crowd as big as it will likely be, Felicia will hardly be in danger of crossing paths with the duke. Though . . ." Ginger paused, girding herself to tread carefully. "Perhaps it's time to tell Fel—"

Ambrosia cut Ginger off crossly. "I'll thank you to keep to your own business. I only informed you of this situation because, in the circumstances, I felt it was my duty. I'll not have it held over my head."

"I apologise," Ginger said sincerely. "If Felicia ever learns the truth, it'll not come from me."

Ambrosia's shoulders slackened as she let out a breath. The matriarch was getting on in years, and Ginger thought the lady looked more tired than usual. The new duke's nuptials and the fact that he and his young bride seemed to be the talk of the town were wearing on her.

"Very well," Ambrosia said. "If you must go, at least return prepared to tell me everything."

"Of course I will, Grandmother." Ginger motioned to the door sitting open to the entrance-way. "Now, please forgive me for not staying longer. The others are waiting."

THE SITTING room was warm with joviality. A wireless took up a large area in the corner, transmitting the popular song "Sonny Boy."

Felicia looked darling in a pink satin crepe gown with an uneven hemline landing just below the knee and a contrasting floral pattern peeking from the underskirt. A blue feather was fixed to a cloche hat and bounced in time to the tapping of Felicia's matching satin shoe. She sat next to Charles on the settee whilst Basil lounged in a matching armchair, all of which faced a large stone fireplace. Long windows let in natural light, creating a sense of warmth, despite the fire being unlit. Ginger admired the two gentlemen, a dapper pair wearing morning coats and black ties, each holding top hats on their laps.

"Darling," Felicia said. "You look divine. And the tea is getting cold. I don't think we have time to ask for another pot."

Basil checked his wristwatch. "We've got a bit of time yet. Brides are notoriously late." He grinned at Ginger, who feigned a pout.

"That was hardly my fault." Ginger lowered herself onto an armchair. "Besides, I wasn't so very late."

"Shall I ring for more tea?" Felicia asked.

"I'm quite all right without." Ginger didn't want to risk spilling or, worse, create a need for the ladies. "Now, what have I missed? You lot seemed to be having a good laugh earlier."

"I was just telling them about that American concoction, Velveeta Cheese," Felicia said.

"Oh yes," Ginger said. "Haley Higgins, told me about it in her last letter."

"Can you imagine?" Felicia waved her fingers. "I can't believe they get away with calling the ghastly stuff cheese. Oh!" Felicia squealed as she reached for Charles' hand. "We're going on another holiday, and Charles is allowing me to choose our destination. Where do you think we should go? A place less dreary than foggy Scotland. I was thinking somewhere more exotic like India or Africa."

Charles shot her a surprised look before offering a stifled chuckle. "I should've known better than to offer carte blanche. I thought perhaps she'd say

France or Switzerland. Surely, you'd prefer a more civilised destination?"

"We've just been to France, darling," Felicia said. "I'm ready for something more adventurous." She clapped her hands. "Ginger, you and Basil should come with us!" With bright eyes, she stared at Basil. "You'd like that wouldn't you, Basil? A safari?"

"Africa is a wild place," Basil answered, "though the adventure could entice me."

"You wouldn't mind us tagging along?" Ginger asked.

Charles languidly crossed his legs. "The more the merrier."

"I could only go when Scout is away at boarding school," Ginger said.

"We shall plan it and have a jolly good time," Felicia returned excitedly.

It was Charles' turn to check his wristwatch. "We really should be tootling. Otherwise, the doors of St. Paul's will be closed to us."

CHAPTER SEVEN

Ginger had been inside St. Paul's Cathedral many times, and each time she felt the same way—awed and slightly overwhelmed. Sir Christopher Wren's baroque structure was breathtaking. The nave felt holy in white marble and gilding, the walls embellished with curlicue relief sculptures. Exquisite, colourful glass mosaics depicting religious themes filled the high vaulted ceilings, so intricate one could spend hours staring at them and not capture every detail. The dome was incredibly captivating and responsible for countless cricks in the neck. The well-known so-called Whispering Gallery encircled the dome, and one had to be extra cautious when sharing secrets there as the design let visitors hear whispers from the other side of the dome. The floor was tiled dramatically in black and white. One couldn't be faulted for believing the church had been built by the hand of God and not by mere mortals.

Having the good fortune to be seated near the front and along the aisle, Ginger sat between Basil and Felicia, with Charles on Felicia's other side. An organist played Elgar's "Salut d'Amour" as the guests arrived.

Felicia whispered to Ginger, "I can't believe Grandmama didn't want to come to this. You did offer her an invitation, too, did you not?"

"I did," Ginger said.

"She's not one to miss out on a social spectacle." Felicia's eyes widened in concern. "She's not unwell, is she? Ginger? She didn't swear you to secrecy?"

"She's as well as she's ever been," Ginger said. Ambrosia had sworn her to secrecy, but not about her health. "However, she is getting on in years and tires more quickly."

Ginger was rescued from further scrutiny by the organist who worked the enormous pipe organ. The vibration from the pipes filled the nave like a deep breath to the lungs, the sound so rich and full one felt it in one's bones.

Felicia whispered to Ginger, "I'm retreating to the gallery now to join the *lads*. I shall snap photographs needed for the magazine and return when I can."

The three lads in question were the other press photographers. From her position under the dome, Ginger could see fellows on the balconies of the north and south transepts standing behind their tripods. Edgar Farley stood out on the north side with his bright red hair. Whilst the other blokes didn't seem to care about having a female in their ranks, Mr. Farley hadn't been as polite. Felicia had confided in Ginger, saying she'd wished to keep her distance from the man to avoid uncomfortable interactions. Ginger noted that Felicia headed out of her way to the south transept to meet this goal.

The organ went quiet, and the sudden silence caught the attention of everyone in attendance. The Bishop of London, Lord Arthur Winnington Ingram entered, and the choirboys took their places in the church quire. The bishop was an elderly man not much older than the groom, but he had far less hair and stood in a manner that suggested he'd been taller as a younger man. He nodded at the groom and his best man seated in the front row, indicating it was time for them to take their places to the right of the altar.

The Duke of Worthington looked dapper in his morning coat, with its long back, white shirt, and silk tie. His hair was white but thick, parted on one side and oiled back.

A hush hovered over the nave as breaths were held, waiting. The organist broke into Wagner's " Bridal Chorus". The bride stepped into view.

Ginger held her breath at the exquisite beauty of her gown. Made of silk, it had smooth, simple lines conforming to a nice figure, but the eye-catching feature was the veil. Many yards of sheer lace flowed from a sequined-embedded head cap, draping behind the bride like a fantastical waterfall—the corners carried by young pageboys. Three brides-maids wearing fashionable gowns ending mid-shin walked in after them.

The duke's eyes were on his bride alone, and in her presence, in this environment, he seemed younger. Ginger felt a dab of shame at having judged them rather harshly. Who was she to doubt the validity of their feelings for one another and ques-tion their love?

The bride arrived at the front, her train sorted neatly by her bridesmaids, who then sat on the bride's side in the front row. The pages had been trained to join the groom's ushers on the groom's side.

Lord Bishop Winnington-Ingram smiled at the full house, opening his arms in welcome.

"Dearly beloved, we are gathered together here in the sight of God, and in the face of this congregation, to join together this man and this woman in holy matrimony, which is an honourable estate, instituted of God in the time of man's innocence, signifying unto us the mystical union that is betwixt Christ and his church."

As the familiar words of the Anglican wedding liturgy washed over Ginger, she was brought back to the vows that she and Basil had shared when they chose to wed. She gave him a knowing smile. He took her hand and squeezed it.

"I require and charge you both," the bishop continued, "as ye will answer at the dreadful day of judgement when the secrets of all hearts shall be disclosed, that if either of you know any impediment, why ye may not be lawfully joined together in matrimony, ye do now confess it. For be ye well assured, that so many as are coupled together otherwise than God's Word doth allow are not joined together by God; neither is their matrimony lawful."

Before either the bride or groom could respond, a deafening sound exploded, reverberating from the curve of the dome. Many men in the congregation ducked for cover, a reflex from the trauma of the Great War, whilst others jumped to their feet, an expression of high alert on their faces. The shrill cry of a woman echoed through the nave, then fell silent.

Ginger grabbed her husband's arm. "Basil?"

He shook his head, already on his feet. The anguished cry of a man—the duke—replaced the stunned silence of the onlookers. Percy Heath, the Duke of Worthington, held the slumped figure of his bride in his arms, a splash of crimson spreading along the back of her white silk gown like the petals of a deadly rose.

CHAPTER EIGHT

In another moment, the cavernous dome echoed with screams and shouting.

Felicia moved her camera away from her eyes and stared down.

After gazing transfixed at the scene at the foot of the stairs, Lord Bishop Winnington Ingram gathered himself. Turning to the congregation, he stretched out his hands, the white sleeves of his surplice billowing.

"Ladies and gentlemen," he called out, his sonorous voice cutting through the clamour. "I beseech you to maintain the peace of the House of God!"

The noise died down as the people turned to his voice of authority.

"Please," the bishop continued, "remain calm."

Felicia swallowed hard at the sight of the bride, crumpled on the ground, unmoving. The red blossom on her gown caused Felicia to believe she'd been shot. She'd chosen to position herself beyond the other photographers, not wanting to deal with their antagonistic gazes. After a slight hesitation, she began snapping photographs, manually advancing the film after each shot. The bride's body first, now reverently laid at the foot of the stairs to the altar, then the groom, the crowd that had gathered, and Basil, with his arm movements, instructing someone to ring Scotland Yard. Slowly, she moved in a circular fashion, snapping the shocked faces of the people, the back of the nave, and around again to the choir area in the front.

The whole while, Felicia's heart hammered in her chest. She was at the scene of an actual crime. She had to find a telephone to let her editor know as soon as possible.

Heading down the stairs, she noticed that the other photographers had taken their shots and left, presumably competing to be the first to crack the story at their papers.

Felicia crept up the north aisle until she came to the front of the church, where a small crowd gathered around the bride's crumpled body.

"Ginger!" she called out in a low voice, trying to

make herself heard over the agitated murmuring of the people in the rows of seats.

Ginger turned, then seeing the camera in Felicia's hands, waved her over. "The police are on their way," she said quietly, "but if you don't mind—it's rather macabre. Or, if you'd rather, I could take a few photographs myself."

"It's not the first time I've seen blood, Ginger," Felicia said. "I can do it." She had brought extra rolls of film and inserted a new one.

Basil sent her a look of regret, and she returned with a small smile of reassurance. "I promise this won't damage my sensibilities."

Basil nodded, then stepped toward the duke, who'd been guided to the front pew and was now sitting with his head in his hands.

Ginger's gaze had followed her husband. "Poor man."

Felicia glanced back too. "What do you think happened?"

"That is yet to be determined," Ginger said. "It's hard to say where the shot came from in this instance, but my guess is from up there." Ginger pointed to the narrow gallery below the dome over the north transept.

"Is there a telephone in the vestry?" Felicia asked.

Ginger frowned. "Why?"

"I need to inform the editor of *The Sketch.*"

"Those photographs are for the police."

"Surely not all," Felicia said. "Yes, these of the body. But others are taken from further away and don't show anything. Ginger, this is my big break!"

"A person has died."

Felicia swallowed. "I'm sorry. I know I'm sounding disrespectful to the dead and to His Grace's grief. But she's already dead. Nothing will change that now."

"If you must ring your editor, you might find a telephone in the Old Deanery."

Felicia prepared her Kodak. "Thank you. I'll be sure to surrender all the photographs to Scotland Yard. But I am going to develop them first. I can finally justify the dark room Charles had built for me."

Felicia hurried away before Ginger could protest. Basil had returned to his wife's side, giving Felicia an opportunity to leave. She needed to find Charles. Her husband was like a ghost when he wanted to be, an expert at blending in and disappearing when it suited him.

GINGER COULDN'T HELP but feel a little unnerved by Felicia's apparent lack of compassion or concern over the death of Miss Wright and her groom's apparent grief. Sometimes, Ginger thought Felicia had finally outgrown her impulsive, childish ways, but today wasn't one of those times. She watched Felicia navigate the crowd, which despite all the clergyman's efforts, had begun to spill out into the aisles, until she disappeared near the back of the cathedral. Ginger doubted she'd be allowed to leave, but hopefully, Charles would spot her and keep his wife from making an attempt.

A commotion near the rear of the nave caught Ginger's attention. The crowd, in their wedding finery, was now dotted with men in uniform, traipsing down the middle aisle, their presence incongruent with the opulence of the cathedral. The stomping of their boots down the black-and-white marble floor echoed in the dome.

Ginger tapped Basil's arm. "The police are here."

One tall, hefty man wearing an oversized trench coat, a thick moustache, and a deep frown lumbered towards them, a felt trilby in hand. Ginger heard Basil muffle a groan, and she nearly emitted one herself. Superintendent Morris had deemed this crime worthy of his attention, presenting himself in person.

Coming to a sudden stop at the steps to the quire of the church, Morris eyed the body on the floor. Without looking at Basil, he barked, "Reed?"

"Murder, sir," Basil returned. "Perpetrator fired a single deadly shot." Basil glanced at Ginger before adding, "I'll speak to the men and organise them."

Ginger lingered as Basil stationed police officers at the entrances, directing them to take the names and addresses of each person present as they were leaving and compare them to the guest lists hastily made available by the duke's staff.

To the superintendent's broad back, Ginger ventured, "We're waiting for the police surgeon to arrive."

Superintendent Morris exhaled as he pivoted slowly towards Ginger's voice. "Mrs. Reed. No doubt I have to remind you, once again, that *this* is police business."

No love was lost between Ginger and the superintendent at Scotland Yard—the two had often been at odds over the years. They'd found a way to coexist, especially since Ginger had undeniably proved to be an asset whilst solving past cases. "I'm a witness," she said simply.

"Very well." Superintendent Morris spoke as if rousing a tad of patience to placate a child. "What did you see?"

Ginger lifted her chin. "Everyone was facing forwards, first to watch the ceremony, and then captivated by the sound of the blast."

"Make way, make way! I'm the doctor!"

A wiry man, who looked as if the weight of his black doctor's bag might topple him over, moved past the last wedding guests waiting their turn with the police. His expression was pensive, his hair slicked back with oil, and his skin was as pasty as if he dwelt primarily in the basement of a hospital.

"Good afternoon, Dr. Wood," Ginger said, motioning to the floor behind her. "The body is this way."

"Good afternoon, Mrs. Reed," Dr. Wood replied. The pathologist and Ginger had crossed paths several times and shared a tenuous rapport due to their mutual dislike of the superintendent. Dr. Wood gave the superintendent a quick nod of acknowledgement before kneeling before the corpse.

"Gunshot," Superintendent Morris offered unnecessarily. "In the back."

"I can see that," Dr. Wood mumbled back.

"Likely from the gallery above. A sniper."

"I gather you're not looking for time of death or means of death," Dr. Wood said with a sigh. "There's no exit wound. I'll retrieve the bullet during the post-mortem." He stood, having completed his duty. "That should help you out, I hope. I'll arrange for the body to be removed."

"Very well," Superintendent Morris growled. He pointed to one of the constables, a familiar face to Ginger. She smiled softly at Constable Braxton, one of Basil's right-hand men, and he smiled in return. "You," Superintendent Morris continued, "arrange to get this cleaned up."

"We'll have to maintain the scene . . ." Ginger interjected. At Superintendent Morris' scowl, she added, "to examine the blood splatter. You were about to say the same thing, weren't you, Superintendent?" She rolled her eyes dramatically. "I'm always speaking out of turn."

"Indeed." Superintendent Morris straightened his tie and turned back to Constable Braxton. "I meant to say, prepare for when it's time to clean this up. Where's the photographer?"

"Sergeant Scott is just behind you now," Constable Braxton said. "He's got his camera at the ready."

Ginger stepped aside to give the police photographer room, secretly pleased that Felicia had been present first. Felicia was probably in her darkroom at Witt House, developing her prints, and Ginger felt a sudden eagerness to go to her, Felicia's previous callousness all but forgotten.

The Duke of Worthington had remained seated all this time, appearing to have gained control of his emotions enough to grant Basil an interview. Ginger came within hearing distance just in time.

"I know this is a very difficult time, Your Grace," Basil said, "but I'm afraid I must ask a few questions. First, can you think of anyone who might've wanted to harm Miss Wright?"

The duke's face pinched with grief. "She was meant to be Lady Worthington by now."

"Yes," Basil said gently. "Again, I offer my condolences. Do you need a bit more time?"

"No, please, let's get this over with." The duke sighed long and hard. "I wish the answer to your question was 'no', Chief Inspector. I'm just trying to think where to begin."

Ginger lowered herself onto the pew not far from the duke. Felicia's photographs would have to wait.

atching the duke's eye, Ginger said gently, "My deepest condolences, Your Grace."

"Thank you, Mrs. Reed." The duke smiled softly. "Your husband has already kindly offered his."

"You inferred that Miss Wright might've had enemies," Basil ventured. Behind his back, he motioned to Constable Braxton and mimed writing in the air. Braxton stepped up, removing a notepad and a short pencil from the pocket of his uniform jacket.

The duke's teary gaze moved from Basil to Ginger and back again. "Perhaps I'm mistaken. Only, Hazel had been acting strangely lately."

"In what way?" Ginger asked.

"She was jumpy. Always glancing over her shoulder as if she thought she was being followed.

When I asked her about it, she laughed, saying the busy wedding schedule had her frazzled." Looking dejected, he added, "I would've gone for a simpler wedding, but . . ."

"But?" Basil pressed.

"Well," the duke shrugged. "Hazel originally wanted a big flashy wedding, going on about how a girl only gets married once, and all that."

"How did you and Miss Wright meet?" Basil asked.

Ginger knew the story, as it had been reported on extensively, but knew that Basil was getting the duke to repeat it for the record. She hated to think the worst of anyone, but many women were killed by the men in their lives each year. Was it possible that the duke had found a way to rid himself of a problem? Before any claims on his wealth could be made, or marks against his character? However, surely he would've just broken off the engagement if that were the case.

"We met at an autumn dance," the duke said. "At first, I thought Miss Wright was merely being polite, staying at my side and engaging in light conversation. Many couples were dancing, and it seemed rude of me not to ask. I expected her to decline, seeing as I am so much older. Plenty of younger men were in the room, but to my great delight, she accepted. We danced three times throughout the evening, and I was so elated by her company—and by the wine that flowed, I suppose—that the minute I got home, I wrote a note of invitation for her to come for tea the next day.

"We saw each other every day. Of course, I was keenly aware of our age difference, but that fact lost its importance over time. I'm vain enough to admit that I began to imagine myself as if I were decades younger."

Ginger shared a look with Basil. The duke hardly seemed like a man trapped in a betrothal with a lady, one that required a desperate means of extraction.

"Does Miss Wright have any family?" Basil asked. "I noticed her side of the aisle was notably empty."

"No," the duke answered with a sigh. "Her family was lost when the ship they were travelling on from America sank. Hazel was lucky to have arrived earlier with her maid, having been sent ahead to finishing school. So much hardship," he added with a deep sigh. "And now this."

"What will you do now?" Ginger asked.

The duke looked up, his eyes dark with grief. "I have my townhouse here in London. I expect the police will need me to stay for a while."

Basil nodded his agreement. "It would be appreciated."

"Then," the duke tugged at his trousers, "I suppose I will head back to my residence." Standing, he smoothed his waistcoat and jacket, soaked red with Miss Wright's blood. "I'm very weary, Chief Inspector. Might we pick this conversation up again in the morning?"

"Of course," Basil said. "Braxton will arrange for officers to accompany you to your motor car. Good day, Your Grace, and again, our deepest sympathies."

WITH THE SUPPORT of his best man, the duke left as his bride-to-be's body was wheeled out on the trolley. Ginger's hand went to her heart in sympathy. The poor man looked as if he'd aged ten years since he'd arrived at the cathedral, and for a man already in advanced years, she was worried about his well-being. Having to face the reporters and crowds of gawkers that would be swarming the cathedral by now certainly didn't help.

Having learned to toughen her emotions through all the tragedies during the war years, Ginger exhaled, threw her shoulders back, and stepped in behind her husband as he approached the quire again.

Now that the body was gone—and thankfully, the ambulance attendants had been careful not to disturb evidence and hadn't carelessly trampled through the blood—the blood splatter patterns were obvious, showing up glaringly across the white and black marble tiles.

"The blood mist is rather fine," Ginger said. She'd witnessed the phenomenon in the war on the uniforms of soldiers who'd been shot from a great distance. "It sprayed on the back of Miss Wright's gown."

"I noticed that too," Basil said. "We can rule out anyone sitting in the front row with an alleged concealed weapon. Otherwise, the blood droplets would be much thicker with a greater amount of forward splatter."

Ginger produced a magnifying glass from her handbag and bent low to examine the small droplets of blood. "The elongated shape and tailing go in this direction." She pointed her finger towards the gallery above. Both she and Basil turned to follow the imaginary trajectory the bullet had to have taken.

"The shot came from the north side," Basil said. "We'll have to wait until Dr. Wood produces the bullet to determine the type of weapon."

"One must presume it's a rifle," Ginger said, "to reach this distance with any accuracy. If we could only see the angle of the bullet's entry into Miss

Wright's back, we could confirm the gunman was on that balcony to take the shot."

"I can't see how the shot could've come from any other position, but it will be nice to get confirmation."

"How long can you keep the public from the cathedral?" Ginger asked, wondering how they could preserve this crime scene.

Basil shook his head. "Not long enough. You might as well go home. I'll be busy at the Yard for some time. Morris has already gone and is waiting for me. I'll get Braxton to drive me home."

"Very well," Ginger said. She was eager to visit Felicia and see how her photographs were developing. And there was Ambrosia to face, who would've heard the news by now.

CHAPTER TEN

What a strange turn of events! Ginger's mind, as she puttered down the lane to the back garden of Hartigan House, was on what was sure to be the crime of the month, if not the season. Here she was, returning alone, with Basil at the Yard, Felicia most likely at home, and Charles. And who knew where he was?

Like all motor cars, the Crossley's engine was louder than the horses and contraptions that still found their place in the streets of London. Its particular rumble was like a proclamation, announcing whenever Ginger was about to arrive. She expected to be greeted by Clement, the gardener and sometimes chauffeur. His face and midsection had grown rounder since he came to serve at Hartigan House, and Ginger had to give Mrs. Beasley, the cook and housekeeper, credit for that. She handed him the keys as she stepped out.

"Do you mind if Marvin parks your motor car, madam?" Clement asked. "He does find tremendous joy in the task, but I can do it if you prefer."

Marvin Elliot spent most of his time tending the two horses in the stable. He'd suffered a brain injury after a nasty fight and could no longer make a living on his own. He was Scout's older cousin, and Ginger had readily given him a room in the attic and a job as Clement's assistant. Like Scout, Marvin had an affinity with horses. He was also fascinated with motor cars.

"I'd be pleased to do it, Mrs. Reed."

Marvin's voice came from behind her. Ginger was pleased to see that his trousers were free from straw, and if he'd been riding that morning, he'd changed out of his riding clothes.

Ginger nodded at Clement, then spoke to Marvin. "Mind the garage doors. Return the key to Clement when you're done."

Removing her gloves as she headed for the house, Ginger spotted Pippins—her faithful former butler—and Boss sitting on the terrace enjoying the early summer sunshine.

"Good afternoon, Pips."

Boss responded by running to her feet, his stubby

tail switching and his black-and-white face breaking into a human-like smile. Ginger knelt to scrub his ears, then swooped him into her arms, finding comfort in the dog's unconditional love and constant exuberance.

"It's a lovely day, madam," Pippins said. Even seated, Pippins was a tall man, though his shoulders, folding with age, had made him less tall than he had been in his youth. He wore a hat over a bald head, and his blue eyes twinkled as he looked at Ginger. "It was a happy wedding, was it?"

"Not all that happy, I'm afraid. I'm sure it's in the news by now. The bride was killed. Murdered."

"Oh mercy."

Ginger was slightly shocked at the elderly butler's use of her favourite phrase. The grim situation made it unseemly, but Ginger couldn't help being amused. She'd never heard Pips say it before. Was it a sign of a diminished mind? She hoped not.

"I need to find Lady Gold, as I must give her the tragic news."

"The dowager is in the sitting room, awaiting your return," Pippins said.

Ginger felt a sense of relief. The man's mind wasn't gone after all. Handing Boss over, she said, "You'll continue keeping an eye on Boss for me, won't you?"

"Certainly, madam. I consider it my duty whilst Master Scout is at boarding school."

Ginger went immediately to the sitting room, where she found Ambrosia pacing in front of the fireplace, her walking stick tapping the floor in an uneven beat.

The elderly matriarch stilled when she saw Ginger, her bulbous eyes growing even rounder as she muttered in horror. "Is it true? Is *she* dead? Mrs. Schofield heard the news from one of her friends who had heard it from someone."

"Have a seat, Grandmother," Ginger said as she rang the bell for tea. "And I'll tell you all about it."

Ambrosia reached for the arm of the nearest chair with a quivering hand, then lowered herself into it. Ginger would've made quick steps to assist her, but she knew that would result in a sharp rebuke. Ambrosia didn't like to be treated like "a frail old lady", even though she fit the description more with each passing year.

Ginger settled into the chair opposite, her eyes moving to *The Mermaid*, a Waterhouse painting her father had once purchased for her mother. The ethereal imagining of the beautiful mythical creature with long red hair conjured up a sense of peace, as if the mermaid stood proxy for her mother, whom she had never got to know.

"Well?" Ambrosia said impatiently. "Am I to die of curiosity?"

"All was going as expected, initially," Ginger said. "The groom was waiting at the altar, though Miss Wright didn't have anyone to walk her down the aisle."

Ambrosia stared incredulously. "She walked it *alone?*"

"Though unusual, it's not unheard of," Ginger said, though it did raise questions about the victim's family connections, or lack of them.

"And then?"

"Before the vows were uttered, a gunshot resounded, and—"

The door to the sitting room opened, and a maid walked in with a tea tray.

"Good Lord," Ambrosia muttered. "Ghastly timing."

"Thank you, Grace," Ginger said, excusing the maid, then beginning to pour a cup each for herself and Ambrosia. Once the sugar and milk were added and stirred, and Ambrosia's cup and saucer handed to her, she continued, "At first, we didn't know if the sound was an actual gunshot, but then Miss Wright crumpled to the floor, face down with a clear bloom of red on her back."

"Oh dear." Ambrosia's hand went to her throat.

"This isn't good at all. Who knows what will be revealed during an investigation? Georgia, you must prevent them from discovering the truth about me."

Ginger blinked. Ambrosia only reverted to Ginger's given name when she was in distress. That she gave little regard to Miss Wright's unfortunate plight was further evidence of the depth of her anxiety.

"You know I can't promise that," Ginger said gently. "A heinous murder has been committed, and justice must be sought."

"At any cost?" Ambrosia said. "Sullying my reputation will not bring that poor girl back. Do you not understand? I cannot be seen as wanton in my youth. The ridicule and scorn will be more than I can bear. And if you have no concern for my feelings, then think of Felicia. She's been through so much torment as a child and has only recently given up her rebellious ways. This, this will be her undoing!"

Ginger sipped her tea with a nod at Ambrosia's neglected cup. Ambrosia took the hint, picked it up, and blew gently before sipping.

"I understand your trepidation," Ginger said. "But I'm afraid Felicia is already in trouble. She's been receiving notes from an anonymous sender who clearly knows the truth about her lineage."

Ambrosia froze with her teacup midair, and Ginger regretted prompting her to drink. After a moment, Ambrosia carefully set the cup and saucer on the table beside her. "I beg your pardon?"

"I didn't mention anything because I didn't want to upset you needlessly," Ginger added. "I'd hoped it was only a single occurrence, even a mistake."

"How many notes have there been?"

Ginger paused, then answered reluctantly. "Three."

"Oh, dear Lord!" Ambrosia's face had blanched, but now a flush of red covered her soft cheeks. "Someone knows. Someone with nefarious intentions!"

"It appears that way."

Ambrosia leaned on her walking stick and locked her round-eyed gaze on Ginger. "What are we to do?"

"I don't know," Ginger said truthfully. "The notes are typed and delivered through the post. Felicia noticed that each postmark is from a different part of London. He or she is very clever."

Ambrosia slumped in her chair. "This is a nightmare."

"I'll do my best to keep your secret," Ginger said, "but Felicia may be in danger, and her welfare comes first."

"Of course it does." Ambrosia looked defeated in a manner that Ginger had never seen before. The dowager was the epitome of a strong-willed lady who had mastered the old ways but floundered in these modern times.

"Ring for Langley," Ambrosia said. "I'm in need of a lie-down."

Ginger waited until Ambrosia's maid arrived to help her mistress up the staircase, then slipped out the front entrance to search for Felicia. It'd been a few hours since she'd disappeared with her rolls of film to develop. Ginger hoped some clue would present itself there.

CHAPTER ELEVEN

Felicia had found Charles in the vestibule of St. Paul's Cathedral. In a rather abrupt manner, he'd taken her elbow and practically pushed her out of the large wooden doors.

"It's best if you just go home," Charles said. "There's a gunman on the loose, and who's to say he won't fire again."

Felicia retorted, "Surely he's not daft enough to start waving a rifle around, especially as he seems to have succeeded in his goal."

"We don't know who his intended target was for certain," Charles said. "It could've been the duke. Miss Wright's death might have been a miss."

Felicia had to concede that Charles had a point, but she hadn't time to elaborate as a row of taxicabs had lined up, summoned by the news that was sure to spread around the city like feathers from a ripped-open pillow. Charles pushed her into one.

"Aren't you coming?" Felicia asked, feeling a little indignant.

"I've offered Basil and the Yard my assistance."

Felicia protested. "But what can you do? You're not a police officer."

Charles either didn't hear or pretended not to hear. "I'll be home shortly." He closed the door and slapped the roof of the taxicab, alerting the driver that he could leave.

With so many leaving simultaneously, it took twenty minutes to get back to Mallowan Court. Felicia used the time judiciously to conjure a list of grievances against her husband. He was secretive and distant. He was neither unpleasant nor uncaring, but Felicia felt like there was an invisible barrier between them . . . and not one constructed by her.

She was an open book. Charles was a bank vault —only opened when he deemed it necessary, and even then, there was no guided tour, just the measured handing out of predetermined currency.

Felicia had Charles physically and intellectually, but she wanted more. She wanted his heart and soul.

Despair washed over her as she anticipated her future. Her role as a supportive wife and nurturing mother—the latter she'd not had a chance to do. At least there had been only one lost child. But why hadn't another come along since then? Felicia wondered if Charles had been doing something to prevent it, but as mysterious and manipulative as he might be, he wasn't yet able to orchestrate the hand of God to his liking. And then guilt pierced her heart. She wasn't entirely unhappy about the postponement of motherhood.

By the time the taxicab parked in front of her house, Felicia had got herself thoroughly riled up. She paid the driver, forgetting to thank him, and marched inside.

"Madam?" Burton appeared at the front door, using that sixth sense that all butlers seemed to possess. He helped her out of her coat. "Is it true? It must be true for you to be home already and without the master."

"I don't know what you've heard, Burton," Felicia said tersely, "but if it has to do with the death of the bride, then yes, it's true. You can inform Lord Davenport-Witt that I'll be in the darkroom when he returns."

"Yes, madam."

Felicia regretted offering that information immediately after it had left her tongue. Charles hadn't been around to see her when she was snapping photographs and didn't know she had two rolls of film in her handbag that needed developing. If he could have secrets, then she could too. Blast it.

That had been hours earlier. It amazed Felicia how quickly time passed when she was working on the developing process. Though tremendous leaps in progress had been made in photography, it was still a long, laborious process from start to finish, all in a lightless room with only the glow from a single red bulb to illuminate the area. She transferred the first roll of film into a light-tight developing tank, then carefully unrolled it and wound it onto a developing wheel before returning it to the developing tank. Carefully, she poured hydroquinone, a developing agent, into the tank, ensuring the film was completely submerged, and gently agitated the tank to ensure even development. Taking a deep breath, she repeated the process with the second roll.

Processing film was a delicate process, and an art in itself, really, and Felicia followed the instructions she'd learned to a T, not wanting to risk spoiling what might be career-defining images.

It was time to transfer the film to a stop bath solution of acetic acid to end the developing process. Having prepared a fixing bath of sodium thiosulfate, Felicia placed the film into a cleansing solution until only the developed image was left. It then needed to be washed and air-dried. Releasing another long breath, she felt satisfied with her work.

Felicia headed for the drawing room to ring for tea whilst she waited, her stomach demanding attention. A maid came shortly with cucumber sandwiches and cake, which Felicia washed down with a cup of tea.

"Lord Davenport-Witt hasn't returned, has he?" Felicia asked, then added quickly to seem only slightly curious about her husband's whereabouts, "I've been in the darkroom for ages; he could've come and gone for all I was aware."

"If he has, madam, he hasn't come hungry."

Felicia finished her tea and returned to the dark room to begin the fun part. With the film developed, she could create prints by placing the developed film directly on a sheet of light-sensitive photographic paper and exposing it to light, with the reverse image transferred. More bathing of the image in developer, stop bath, and fixing solutions ensued until the final image was finally clipped to a line in the dark room and hung to dry. At the end of this process, Felicia heard a knock on the door, followed by a familiar voice.

"Felicia? Are you in there? It's me, Ginger. Can I come in?"

· · ·

GINGER WAITED in the darkness of the two-door system that ensured no light could enter the darkroom when the main door was opened. Hearing Felicia grant her permission to enter, Ginger moved into the red-lit room. As she'd hoped, Felicia was already at the point of hanging the photographs to dry, the images imprinted on the paper growing more apparent with each passing moment. There were so many images that the room looked decorated with a banner of many small white flags, and Ginger had to duck to be careful not to run into any of them. "You've been busy," she said.

"Well, I don't have an active household or children or a husband who allows me to be part of his life," Felicia returned without looking up. "I don't even have Grandmama to spar with, so what else am I to do with my time?"

Ginger was surprised by the thread of vitriol in Felicia's voice. She was usually the cheery, happy-go-lucky sort, but clearly, she was unhappy with Charles. Ginger had no desire to get involved in the drama between husband and wife, so she diverted to the dowager Lady Gold.

"We could arrange for Grandmother to move in with you."

"Ha!" Felicia said, pinning the final photograph to the wire strung across the room. "She was pure misery when we moved her from Chesterton. That lady doesn't like change, and it wouldn't be fair to her at her advanced age to do that to her now."

"But think of how much fun you'd have with her renewed cantankerousness. It would make a good match for yours."

Felicia scowled, the red light casting shadows that emphasised her frown lines. "I'm not tetchy."

"Then tell me what's going on," Ginger said gently. "You seem out of sorts."

Felicia sighed. "It's nothing. Just a lot of small things adding up to something bigger. Those notes, the wedding, the shooting . . ."

Felicia's sentence fell off, but Ginger could guess the unspoken source of angst. *Charles.*

"Let's look at what you've got here," Ginger said, hoping to distract Felicia from her woes. "You've got a good eye. Better than the police photographer, I bet."

"You needn't mollify me. I had the good fortune of being there when the crime took place. It's natural I'd have more photographs."

Ginger sensed that she couldn't win with Felicia in her current mood and focused instead on the images themselves. "These are developing nicely," she said.

Felicia nodded her agreement. She followed

Ginger as she examined each one. What became clear to her was a particular person who transcended time and space to appear in many shots. Ginger glanced at Felicia, whose frown had deepened even more. She saw it too.

"Felicia?"

"I see him, Ginger. Charles! How is it he's in so many of the photographs? It's like I was following his path, but I wasn't. At least not consciously." She stared hard at Ginger. "He circled up to the balcony, encircled the dome, came down the stairs to the nave, then along the side aisle back to the altar. What was he looking for?"

Or whom? Ginger thought.

"Oh, Ginger." Felicia's eyes welled up with tears. "It's like I married a ghost. I don't even know my own husband."

Oh mercy. Ginger faced Felicia. "I'm sure there's a perfectly good reason for it all. It's probably nothing more than his wanting to aid the police, checking on things until they arrived. Charles is very resourceful that way."

Felicia hiccupped and held a palm to her mouth. "You're probably right. I'm just being a silly, emotional female. I don't know what's wrong with me. I imagine Charles has a completely other life that's far more interesting than the one he has with me. I'm jealous about nothing. It's a wonder Charles puts up with me at all."

Ginger patted Felicia's arm, wishing she could comfort her. Felicia was more discerning and observant than Ginger gave her credit for. Between Charles and Ambrosia, the secrets and lies were a mounting fortress, one Ginger didn't know if she could keep hiding. She'd expose them both if she could have her way, but that wouldn't be fair to Felicia. Sometimes the truth didn't set one free. Better Felicia existed in a world that was safe for her, even if it wasn't transparent.

"Why don't we have a chat whilst we let these dry?" Ginger said, guiding Felicia towards the door. "I'd love to hear about your plans for the back garden."

CHAPTER TWELVE

That evening in the sitting room, Ginger lingered with Basil over a glass of brandy; she sensed her husband's frustration with the Worthington case.

"I can't even narrow it down to one good suspect," he said with tight lips. "None of the guests stand out as a possibility. The bridesmaids' connection with the bride turned out to be superficial. The duke's ushers were of exemplary character. Besides, a single shot from that distance had to be the work of a professional."

"Hired by one of the guests?"

"That's my guess."

"Have the three photographers been cleared?" Ginger asked.

"All but Farley. He had misdemeanour charges

due to his inability to control his anger in public. I'll have him brought in for further questioning tomorrow. He can't be ruled out, but he's just one of hundreds of people who were present."

"You mustn't be too hard on yourself or your men," Ginger said kindly. "This is a difficult case."

"The strange thing about this case, Ginger, is the victim." Basil leaned forward, propping an elbow on one knee. "Miss Hazel Wright was supposedly the orphaned child of an industrialist from America, though there's no official record to support this claim. In fact, it appears to be fabricated. I'm starting to believe this case might have an international component, in which case, it will be taken out of my hands whether I like it or not."

Ginger's heart skipped a beat. "Are you thinking espionage?"

Basil relaxed into his chair. "It's not beyond the scope of possibility. Everyone knows the British secret service was active during the war . . ." He paused, holding Ginger's gaze with his own.

Ginger simply glanced away. She was fairly certain Basil had guessed her involvement, but she was still bound morally and legally by the Official Secrets Act to stay silent on the matter.

Basil continued, "There's no reason to believe

such activities have ceased just because the war has ended."

Ginger looked back. "So, who's the spy? Hazel Wright or the duke?"

"That's a good question." Basil sipped his drink. "The point is, if our government is responsible, this case is already closed. If another government is responsible, there will be difficulties between the Crown and the interfering country, all of which are beyond the scope of my employment."

Frowning, Ginger said, "So it's finished, then? Is your involvement in the case over?"

"Not yet, not officially. But I wouldn't be surprised if Morris asked me to drop it."

"How do you feel about that?"

"Dreadful. It's hardly justice to Miss Wright. Whoever she may have actually been."

Ginger rested her head on the back of the wingback chair and closed her eyes. If Basil was correct and there was more to this shooting than met the eye, it could all be swept under the proverbial carpet. It wouldn't be the first time Ginger had witnessed the phenomenon.

"You're tired, love," Basil said. "Let's go to bed and leave these problems for the morning." He got to his feet and offered Ginger a hand. She was eager to comply. A good night's sleep would be welcomed, especially since she sensed this particular problem wouldn't easily be swept away.

EARLY THE NEXT MORNING, Ginger closed herself in the privacy of her study and rang the office of Lady Gold Investigations. Her assistant, Magna Jones, was an early riser and often went to the office early, a pattern Ginger was pleased held true that morning.

She breathed a short breath of relief when the call was connected. "Magna, it's me. I have an assignment for you."

Magna Jones had worked with Ginger as a secret service agent during the war. She was skilled and experienced at watching a target and following discreetly. She had recently acquired a nondescript, black motor car which aided her immensely. Magna had short, dark hair smoothed back with hair oil, piercing dark eyes, and a hard look that could make a grown man quiver in his boots. She reminded Ginger of a black panther, lithe and quiet, and if it hadn't been for good laws in place, she'd be wild and wanton. These qualities had made her an excellent agent during the war and now an exceptional, if overqualified, assistant.

When she had finished her morning tea, Ginger checked her wristwatch, then walked to the entrance to peer out of one of the tall windows flanking the front door. Parked at the entrance of the cul-de-sac was Magna's motor car. As if on cue, Charles exited his house and hopped into his motor car which his driver had brought around for him and sped away. Magna waited a couple of seconds before pulling in behind him. Ginger had warned her that Charles was as skilled as they were and would notice if he was followed too closely.

Magna had reassured her. "I'll stay two vehicles back."

Satisfied, Ginger entered the morning room for breakfast and found Basil and Ambrosia there. "Good morning," Ginger said.

Ambrosia ducked her chin. "Good morning."

Basil looked up over his cup of tea. "You were up early."

"I couldn't sleep," Ginger said as she prepared her plate.

Mrs. Beasley always had a delicious breakfast of eggs, fried bacon and sausages, and slices of grilled tomatoes and mushrooms.

"I spent some time playing with Rosa before she went back to sleep," Ginger continued, "then did a bit of work. The summer line is fabulous, and I have a lot of fabrics and ready-to-wear items to order for Feathers & Flair."

Having filled her plate, she sat beside Basil and across from Ambrosia. "How are you, Grandmother?" Ginger asked. "Did you sleep well?"

"I did not. How can one sleep when the world is so dangerous one can't even get married safely in a church? Especially in St. Paul's Cathedral!"

"I'm sure this is an extraordinary circumstance," Ginger said.

A low whine by her feet caused Ginger to look down. Boss, on his haunches, stared up with round, hopeful brown eyes. "Going to church is probably one of the safest things a person can still do," Ginger said as she slipped her pet a piece of bacon. Turning to Basil, she asked, "Is there any word from Superintendent Morris?"

Basil shook his head. "Not yet. Perhaps some new clue concerning the case will fall onto my desk today. Wouldn't that be spectacular?"

Ginger buttered her toast. "It most certainly would. You mentioned you'd be interviewing Mr. Farley today."

"Indeed." Basil cocked his head. "Would you like to watch?"

Ginger grinned. She'd been privileged to stand in the listening room before. "I do believe I can clear my diary this morning."

After breakfast, she spent more time with little

Rosa, then drove her Crossley to Scotland Yard—putting the rubber ball of her horn to good use.

Ginger walked the corridors of Scotland Yard with the confidence of one who belonged there, even if it meant ignoring the dismayed looks of certain force members. They knew better by now not to be disparaging when it came to Chief Inspector Basil Reed's wife. Superintendent Morris might have had something to do with that. Ginger and the superintendent weren't friends. They weren't even friendly, but they'd come to an unspoken truce.

Meeting Basil at his office, she walked with him to an interrogation room and entered the small space with a covered window looking in as Basil continued into the main room.

Mr. Farley was already seated. In his mid-thirties, the man already had a forehead full of wrinkles, a determined, brown-eyed stare, and yellowed fingers from an apparent nicotine habit. "Do I need to ring my solicitor?" he asked without preamble.

"That's up to you," Basil said, sitting across the table from the photographer. "I'm trying to solve the murder of Miss Wright, and I'm hoping you'll grant me your cooperation. The other photographers have already given their statements."

"Well, if that's all you want, a blasted statement,

then all right." He aggressively tapped his wrist-watch. "But I don't have all day."

"Only a few photographers were granted access to the wedding," Basil started. "How did you become one of them?"

Mr. Farley sniffed. "I have seniority at my paper. First right of refusal and all that."

Basil leaned back. "You don't seem the type to shoot society weddings."

"I certainly don't. What man does? But it's a job."

"You made it clear that you didn't appreciate Lady Davenport-Witt joining your ranks."

"Now look here, Chief Inspector. I know you're like family with Lord and Lady Davenport-Witt. I do my homework too. But lady or not, she had no right to be on that balcony in the gallery."

"Because she's female?"

"That, yes. And she bought that expensive camera? That qualifies her?"

"She was hired to be there by *The Sketch* magazine. She had every right as you had."

Mr. Farley slapped his leg. "Fine. What's that got to do with anything, anyway?"

"It shows that you're antagonistic towards women."

"Oh, so I don't care for women, so I'm going to shoot the bride of some dusty duke? Give me some credit, Chief Inspector." Mr. Farley ran a hand through his red hair. "You want a statement from me? Here it is. I went to work on a job because of the cash offered and got more than I bargained for when I snapped a few photos. Which, by the way, I dutifully submitted to the police for evidence."

Ginger acknowledged the truth of that statement. Basil had expressed frustration that nothing of import had come from viewing the photographs.

"Now," Mr. Farley continued, "if you're not going to arrest me, I'll be on my way."

Basil waved a palm. "You're free to go."

He watched as the photographer left, then turned to the one-way glass, giving Ginger a helpless shrug. Ginger empathised. This was a difficult case, and one that might not be solved.

After a few minutes consoling Basil, Ginger left him at his desk and drove to Regent Street to check up on Feathers & Flair.

She loved her shop with its high ceilings trimmed in mouldings painted gold and the electric crystal lamps. The windows presented mannequins dressed in the latest fashions, and a staircase led to an upper level where factory designs were displayed and sold.

"Bonjour, madame!" The shop manager, Madame

Roux, greeted her with a big smile, as she did every day, as if she hadn't seen Ginger in weeks. A slender woman in her fifties, she dressed tastefully but not ostentatiously, as she'd never want to outshine a potential customer. She had the energy of a much younger woman and approached Ginger along the white marble floor with a spring in her step. "Such a nice arrival today," she added enthusiastically. "The girls are in the back, simply enamoured."

With Boss in the crook of her elbow, Ginger traipsed across the tiled floor to the red velvet curtain that separated the front of the shop from the back. Three youthful, well-coiffed heads turned when Ginger slipped through the curtain.

"Mrs. Reed, come and see." Emma, Ginger's top-notch designer, motioned with her skilled hands. Ginger placed Boss on the floor, and he promptly went to his basket—conveniently for the little dog, Ginger had had many made and placed strategically around both her home and workplace.

"The fabric is from India," Dorothy said, her eyes round. Dorothy was in charge of the upper floor, displaying the factory-made frocks and accessories. Ginger had to assume that the area had no customers. Madame Roux would be certain to call for Dorothy when necessary. Millie, the salesgirl and sometimes model, had opened the new arrivals of factory-made frocks. "These are gorgeous, and I love the convenience," she said, "but how embarrassing to run into someone else wearing the same dress."

"London is large enough," Dorothy said, coming to the defence of her department. "It's unlikely to happen, and even if it did, the affordability and ease are worth it to many ladies."

As if just remembering, Millie stared at Ginger. "Weren't you at that wedding, Mrs. Reed? At St. Paul's Cathedral?"

Ginger nodded. "Indeed I was."

"Is it true that the bride was shot?" Emma asked.

Ginger nodded again.

"The poor lady," Emma mourned, "and her poor gown. You must've seen it, Mrs. Reed. Was it beautiful?"

"Very beautiful, but certainly not the real tragedy."

"Of course," Emma said quickly. "Do the police know who did it?"

This time Ginger shook her head. "Not yet."

"Blast it," Dorothy muttered, shocking them all. "A girl can't even get married in peace anymore. Is there no safe place for us?"

Ginger didn't have the heart to chastise the young woman for her crassness because she wasn't wrong. The gentler sex couldn't count on protection from men and were often prey.

"It's not known if the person who fired the gun is male or female," Ginger said fairly.

Millie wrinkled her nose. "A woman firing a gun?"

"There are plenty of women who are skilled with a rifle." Ginger didn't elaborate, but her mind went to several women she'd met throughout the war who qualified as skilled marksmen.

"Farmers' wives and those in the north," Dorothy said, oblivious to the judgement in her statement.

Madame Roux stepped in. "Dorothy, a customer has just gone upstairs. Millie, another is on the floor. You'll have to save your admiration for the new products until later."

Ginger was relieved to have the conversation stopped. "If you need me, Madame Roux, I'll be in the office reviewing the books."

Her manager ducked her chin and then disappeared behind the velvet curtain.

After completing her paperwork, Ginger took lunch at the cafe across the street, then walked with Boss around the corner to the office of Lady Gold Investigations. The office, in the basement of the building, had once been a shoe repair shop. Ginger had had the entire space redecorated, and even though one had to take a few steps down from pavement level, there was enough light from the window and newly installed electric lights to make it feel warm and bright.

She stepped through the small waiting area into the open office space and moved to her desk. She put a bit of ham she'd saved from her sandwich into Boss' bowl near his basket by the wall, then removed her coat and gloves.

Magna joined her from the kitchenette down the corridor with a tray of coffee and two cups. Ginger's assistant had an uncanny way of anticipating things, including, it turned out, Ginger's arrival. "Oh good, you're finally here." Magna wasn't the type to waste time on pleasantries. "I have news."

CHAPTER THIRTEEN

The bell above the door rang before Magna could get another word in. Both she and Ginger turned towards the sound. Ginger wondered if another client had wandered in, but instead, the familiar form of Felicia stepped through the doorway. She struck a pose, wearing a light coat, accented with fur trim and matching cap, looking every bit a Lady, but her expression was anything but pleased.

Ginger got to her feet. "Felicia? What's happened?"

Felicia waved a small white card. "It's another blasted note!" Then, as if remembering her manners, she nodded to Magna. "Good day, Miss Jones."

Magna nodded in kind. "Lady Davenport-Witt."

Ginger considered the two ladies in her

company. They couldn't have been more different, yet Felicia had been Magna's predecessor, having worked as Ginger's assistant before her marriage. She wondered if this had anything to do with the apparent coolness between them. Or perhaps she was reading too much into it.

Ginger reached out her hand. "Let me see it."

Felicia handed the note over.

Lady Davenport-Witt,

Thieves, however cunning, must have their recompense. I gave you back what was yours. Now you must do something for me. Unless you want the world to know your dark secret.

Ginger noted a slight key misalignment in the text. The *k* skipped ahead slightly in the words "back" and "dark", leaving a wider space between it and the letter before it. This could be a clue to the sender's identity that the other notes—which only used the letter k at the beginning of the word "know"—hadn't provided.

"I have no idea what this means!" Felicia cried. "What dark secret? What did this person give back to me? I feel like I'm about to go crazy."

"Have a seat," Ginger said gently. As she guided Felicia to the nearest leather armchair situated in front of her desk, she glanced at Magna. "Would you mind getting a cup for Lady Davenport-Witt?"

Magna stared back blankly, hesitating before she pushed away from her own desk. Ginger knew she didn't like menial work or anything that made her feel like a servant, but providing refreshments for their clients was part of her job as the assistant. Perhaps she didn't yet see Felicia as a client. That was about to change.

"Bossy," Ginger said, rousing her sleepy dog. "You've been very rude. Stop being so lazy and say hello to Felicia."

Boss sniffed and, with that sixth sense that canines seemed to possess, seemed to understand that Felicia was in distress and in need of comfort. He stood, stretched out his short hind legs and went immediately to Felicia's side, nudging her leg with his nose.

"Oh, Boss," Felicia said, her face breaking into a smile for the first time. "You really do know how to bring cheer." She scratched his ears and then patted his head. His furry presence seemed to soothe her, and she finally took a long breath and relaxed her shoulders.

Magna arrived with a third cup, and set it on Ginger's desk, letting her pour.

"Am I making too much of these?" Felicia said

after a sip. "Should I just throw them into the bin when they come and not give them another moment of my time and attention?"

"No," Ginger said quickly. "One never knows if it will be necessary to produce them."

"Produce them for whom?" Felicia said with concern. "The police?"

"Give them to me," Ginger said calmly, "as a precaution. But hopefully this writer will grow weary and stop. Especially since you are ignoring him."

"Or her," Magna interjected. "Women have devious minds, and poison pen letters often come from a female hand."

Ginger corrected herself. "Or her." She held out the note to Magna, and her assistant took it.

After reading, Magna looked up, her eyes steely with indignation. "And there are more?"

"Two more," Felicia offered. "Well, three, but I stupidly threw the first one away. This is the fourth."

"The others are of a similar ilk?" Magna asked. Felicia nodded, and Magna added, "Can I see them?"

"I don't have them," Felicia said, looking at Ginger.

"Love," Ginger said, taking Felicia's empty cup. "The summer shipment from Paris has just arrived at Feathers & Flair. The latest Lucien Lelong would look tremendous on you. Why don't you let me ponder this problem whilst you go and do a bit of shopping."

Felicia's eyes moved from Ginger to Magna and back, her lips tightening. Ginger's offer was mildly condescending, and Felicia was no empty-headed beauty. The look in her eyes was calculating, as if she knew Ginger was purposely trying to be rid of her so she could speak to Magna without her present. Just when Ginger thought Felicia would protest, she flashed a flat smile. "Yes, driving up my account at your shop will make me feel better." She put on her gloves, clutched her handbag, and then stood. "Thank you for the coffee and for considering my little problem. Have a good day, ladies."

"I don't think she appreciated being dismissed," Magna said. "And I can't wait to hear why you thought it was necessary."

Ginger opened the desk's top drawer, pulled out two cards like the one in Magna's hand and slid them towards her, the first to arrive pushed ahead a little.

Magna picked up the nearest one and read aloud. "Dearest Lady Davenport-Witt. Your name was GOLDen, but what is its real WORTH? The truth is stranger than fiction. Do you really want to know it?

I do." Magna raised a brow. "*Gold* as in your family name? *Worth* as in Worthington?"

Ginger simply shrugged.

Magna huffed, then read the next one. "Dearest Lady Davenport-Witt. Does one really know who one is? Do you know who you are? The truth sets one free. Or does it cheat and steal and imprison?" Magna chortled. "It appears Lady Davenport-Witt has Worthington blood." She stared at Ginger. "I can't believe she hasn't figured this out."

"It's easier when you can be objective," Ginger said, not bothering to deny it. If she wanted to find the writer of these nasty notes, she'd need Magna's help. "There's no delicate way to say this," she started regretfully. "Felicia's father was Robert Gold. However, Robert Gold was not the offspring of Ambrosia's late husband, Artemis Gold."

"How do you know this?" Magna asked. "Don't tell me the dowager actually confides in you."

"Not without good reason." Ginger pushed a lock of her red bob behind her ear, causing her dangling diamond-and-emerald earring to swing. "And in this instance, her duty triumphed over self-preservation. However, I do believe she deeply regrets being honourable now."

"Is your husband aware of these facts?"

"I've recently informed him. I regret breaking my

promise to keep Ambrosia's secret, but these notes make me believe a murder happened as a result."

Magna frowned. "A killer who kills once might kill again."

"I know." Ginger shared Magna's concern. "Felicia may be in danger. Perhaps I shouldn't have sent her out alone." She picked up her telephone receiver and rang Feathers & Flair. When the operator connected her to Madame Roux, Ginger asked, "Does Lady Davenport-Witt happen to be there?"

"*Oui,* madame," the voice returned. "The lady has just walked in. Shall I fetch her?"

"No, that's all right," Ginger said, feeling a bit silly. "I'll catch up with her later."

Magna collected the empty cups and saucers. "Let me get these out of our way, and when I get back, I'll tell you what I learned about Lord Davenport-Witt."

Oh mercy. With Felicia's unexpected arrival and troubling announcement, Ginger had forgotten about Magna's report. "Do hurry."

CHAPTER FOURTEEN

"Stop holding me in suspense," Ginger said with a note of exasperation. "What did you find out?"

Magna smiled slyly, clearly enjoying that she currently held the cards. "Well," she started slowly, "he drove his motor car to the House of Lords, a little disappointing at first, I admit. He parked and went inside. I thought it would be a long, boring wait, but lo and behold, just ten minutes later, he stepped outside. I waited for him to go to his motor car, but he waved down a taxicab instead."

"Interesting," Ginger mused. "Though, I hear that some people find London a stressful city to drive in."

Magna's eyes flashed with amusement. "Unlike you, or myself for that matter. But no, I don't think that's why the earl hailed a taxicab. I followed the taxi, and he got out at Pimlico and entered a public house."

Ginger thought she knew the establishment.

"Terribly uninteresting," Magna continued, "but when he got out, he'd changed his clothes to look like a commoner."

"Another disguise?" Ginger said, wondering what on earth Charles could be up to. "Then what?"

"Lord Davenport-Witt circled the area on foot, not stopping until he reached a Soviet club."

"A Soviet club?" Ginger couldn't help the shock in her voice. After the war, Britain had broken diplomatic relations with the Soviet Union, but a few clubs still supported the ideology in London. "Did he go inside?"

Magna's lips spread across her face as if she were holding in a chuckle. "He certainly did. He's either a Soviet sympathiser or . . ." She pushed dark hair behind her ears as she narrowed her steely eyes. "Is it possible, Ginger, that your brother-in-law has more in common with you, with us, than you are aware of? Or . . ." She raised a thinly plucked dark brow. "You *are* aware but didn't care to share with me?"

When Ginger failed to deny it immediately, Magna burst out loudly, "Aha!"

Ginger slumped in her chair. "That's hardly necessary. I didn't admit or deny anything. Charles could've gone to the Soviet club for any number of reasons."

"Very well," Magna said. "Your earl is the epitome of innocence and naivety."

Oh mercy.

"Or," Magna continued, "you'd rather protect him than find Miss Wright's murderer."

Ginger bit back rising anger. "It's possible to do both."

Magna laughed. "So, he *is* more than a boring lord."

"You can think what you like," Ginger said. "I'm not commenting either way, not until it becomes imperative that I do."

"Fair enough."

"If the earl is acting as an agent, the question is—what does the Soviet club have to do with the dead bride?"

"I thought you might ask that," Magna said as she put her feet on her desk, crossing her T-strap shoes at the ankles. If her assistant were to be caricatured as a bird, Ginger would describe her as a crow. Brilliant and conniving, believing she was better than other birds, and not afraid to dig through rubbish.

"I spent some time at the Public Record Office searching for background information on Hazel Wright, and there's nothing conclusive to report. At least not this one. There are older ones, and married ones, and divorced ones."

"Do you think she's Russian?" Ginger asked.

"It's not unthinkable. Just because the war is over doesn't mean intelligence agencies are asleep at the wheel." She cocked her head. "I find it interesting that the earl's wife is getting nuisance notes implicating a connection with the duke. Rather a lot of coincidences at work, wouldn't you agree?"

"I would," Ginger said. "I'm not a fan of coincidences." She caught Magna's steely stare. "What do you suggest our next move should be?"

"If I were you, I'd have a good talk with Felicia's husband."

Ginger had had the exact same idea. "My thoughts exactly." She stood and gathered her things. "I hope he's returned to the House of Lords."

"Is he aware that Felicia may be in danger?"

Ginger stilled. "I don't know, but I intend to ensure he does."

"Very good," Magna said. "I'll man the fort."

"Fabulous. Will you look after Boss?" Ginger and Magna both darted a look at Boss, who'd slept through everything.

"Of course," Magna said. "Do you think he'll keep sleeping? I'm not a great dog walker."

"Actually, I'll ask Felicia to take him home,"

Ginger said. "It's an excuse to get her out of the streets of London."

The bell on the office door chimed as Ginger left, Boss in her arms. She strolled purposefully down the street and around the corner onto Regent Street. Her timing was perfect. She caught Felicia as she was leaving with two large shopping bags. Ginger waved down a taxicab.

"I'll do it only because I'm fond of Boss," Felicia pouted. "And that my feet are killing me."

"You need to stop buying shoes a size too small," Ginger said lightly. "They don't make your feet look any smaller."

"Says someone with dainty feet," Felicia grumbled as she entered the black taxicab.

Ginger protested. "I don't have dainty feet."

"Where are you off to that you can't return your pet to Hartigan House?"

"Nowhere interesting."

Ginger wasn't certain how she was going to track down Charles. A man like that could be anywhere, but her best bet was the House of Lords. If she couldn't find him there, perhaps she'd run into someone who knew where he could be found.

Ginger drove through Piccadilly and Whitehall

to the Palace of Westminster along the River Thames, parking nearby. There were plenty of people milling about. In their hats and overcoats, gentlemen walked purposefully, as if pressing into the wind. Ladies strolled languidly, some pushing prams, taking advantage of the sunny weather. Newsboys, in their flat caps, stood on opposite corners selling their newspapers.

Ginger gave the lad nearest the Palace of Westminster two pence and took a newspaper. Newspapers were terrific guises to make loitering acceptable and hide one's face if necessary. Miss Wright's death and the duke's plight had moved down below the fold, but the news remained on the first page. Ginger perused the article, a rehashing of what everyone already knew. The gunman remained at large and unidentified. No motives were known, and Scotland Yard continued to be stubbornly mum.

Finally, Ginger's patience paid off, and Charles came out of the House of Lords. He was a good way down the wide pavement, walking away from her when she called out. "Lord Davenport-Witt!"

Charles turned, his eyes widening with recognition. "Mrs. Reed?"

Naturally, the two were on first-name basis in a familiar setting, but in public, they stayed with their formal address. Charles walked quickly towards her.

"Is there trouble?" When he drew close enough to speak quietly, he asked "Is my wife all right?"

Ginger felt a burst of alarm that Charles' first assumption was that Felicia was in danger.

"As far as I know," she said coolly. "Is there a reason why you think she might be in harm's way?"

"No, no," Charles returned with a forced chuckle. "I was just surprised when you called my name so dramatically."

"Charles." Ginger had no choice now but to call a spade a spade. "I know."

Charles cast a glance around them, ensuring they could not be overheard. "Know what?"

"I *know*. And now that Felicia may be in danger, we must drop pretences."

Charles pinched his lips together and gave a slight nod. "Did you bring your motor car?"

"Yes."

"Pick me up at King Charles Street arch. We can talk freely then." Loudly, he added, "Very nice to see you again, Mrs. Reed. Please give my regards to your good husband."

As Charles had suggested, Ginger drove the short distance down Parliament Street to the monument, the white sculpted arches over King Charles Street, completed not long after the turn of the century. Slow traffic had caused her arrival to coincide with

Charles' long gait, and she pulled up as he arrived. She stopped long enough for Charles to fold himself into the passenger seat and pulled back into traffic. "Where to now?"

"Just drive about," Charles said with a flick of his hand. "We can talk whilst you drive."

That suited Ginger. However, after slamming on her brakes several times for reckless drivers on her way down King Charles Street towards St. James's Park and cutting Charles off mid-sentence to squeeze the bulb of her horn, Charles placed a hand on the dash and said tightly, "Let's go for a walk after all! Enter the park and stop."

Ginger cut the steering wheel sharply, entered the park immediately, and took the first available spot to park her motor car.

"Good Lord, Ginger," Charles gasped. "You nearly clipped that lamp post."

Ginger stretched her neck to look out of Charles' window. "Nonsense. There's plenty of room."

Charles stared at Ginger with a look of disbelief. "I can't understand why Basil lets you drive."

"Basil doesn't *let* me do anything. Besides, I can't help it if London is filled with bad drivers. Now, shall we remain in the car or go for a stroll?"

"We shan't be long," Charles said. "Let's say what

we must and then go our own ways. I'm sure you must still have plenty to do today."

"As must you." Ginger swivelled to face Charles. "Are you aware of Felicia's connection with the Duke of Worthington?"

Charles blinked hard. "What do you mean?"

"I mean, I know you have, er, connections. Have you learned anything about Felicia's connection with the duke?"

"Perhaps you should tell me what you know, Ginger."

Ginger no longer saw the point of holding her cards to her chest. She told Charles about the nuisance writer.

"She never mentioned these notes to me," he returned with a note of indignation. Ginger didn't think it prudent to point out that Charles spent much time away from home.

"Felicia doesn't understand the significance of them."

"The writer has reason to think Felicia's connected with the Duke of Worthington, and so, apparently, do you. For the sake of Felicia's well-being, please tell me what you know."

Ginger sighed, feeling a weight at how many times she'd had to relay this sorry tale. "The sad truth is, the dowager Lady Gold had a dalliance with the former Duke of Worthington when they were both very young. Sir Artemis Gold raised the resulting child as his own."

"I see," Charles said quietly.

"The current Duke of Worthington is Felicia's great uncle."

"Is Felicia aware of this?"

"She is not, but I think she's starting to suspect something is amiss."

After a long pause, Charles said, "This is very troubling. Whoever shot Miss Wright could be the writer of these notes." He shot Ginger a look. "Where is Felicia now?"

"I believe she's at home."

"Can I trouble you to make sure?"

"Of course." Charles reached for the door handle, but Ginger stopped him before he could hop out. "Charles, is something or someone at the Soviet club key to this case?"

Charles locked eyes with her. "I'm afraid I could only tell you if you really needed to know. I'm sure you, of all people, understand."

"The Soviet clubs springing up across the country are a cause for concern," Ginger pressed. It was a sentiment often expressed in the newspapers. "I can see why the crown would want to infiltrate."

"Yes, well, until you agree to rejoin the service,

I'm afraid I can say no more." Charles smiled stiffly as he stepped out. "Good day, Ginger. Please ring the House of Lords to let me know Felicia is safe. Don't alarm her by suggesting that she do it. I'll be back at Witt House shortly."

"Would you like a lift?" Ginger asked. "It would be faster than walking."

This time Charles' smile was genuine. "Thank you, but I believe I'd rather walk."

CHAPTER FIFTEEN

Felicia delivered Boss into Pippins' care, then strolled across the cul-de-sac to her home, where Burton greeted her.

"Good afternoon, madam," he said stiffly.

"Burton," Felicia returned. The butler looked flushed, and Felicia wondered if the man was unwell. "Is everything all right?"

"Quite, madam," Burton responded.

"Actually, I am quite famished." Felicia had meant to grab a bite to eat in Mayfair before being abruptly ushered home. Ginger often behaved oddly, not always, but at times, and Felicia never understood why. And Burton, instead of taking her coat, which was his typical manner, of course, had disappeared before Felicia could even ring the bell to summon the maid to see to her lunch. The world seemed topsy-turvy, everyone having an adventure but her.

Felicia moved to the sitting room, draped her coat over the back of a chair for a maid or Burton himself to collect later, and flopped onto the settee. Her mind raced as she peeled off her gloves and removed her cloche hat. She felt something important was happening around her and that everyone but herself was privy to it. The last to get the joke. Or perhaps she was the butt of the joke.

After a quick curtsy, Daphne entered and said, "Cook has lunch prepared for you. The dining room is set."

"I'd rather eat in the back garden, on the patio. It wouldn't do to waste a lovely day like today sitting inside."

"Yes, madam." Daphne, spotting Felicia's coat, picked it off the armchair, curtsied again, and hurried out.

With a sense of weariness, Felicia got to her feet and headed upstairs. The place still felt dark and gloomy despite trying to brighten the old house with new furniture and fresh wallpaper. Perhaps that was due to the low number of windows or the odd interior design.

Or, more likely, she felt like she rattled about inside it alone. Since her marriage, Felicia had lost touch with most of her friends, who either remained single and partied wildly or had married and moved on. Ginger was her one and only friend, and she seemed to have a full life bursting with fun and adventure—running her fancy shop or solving intriguing mysteries. On top of that, she had two children to care for and a busy house to manage.

In her bedroom, Felicia stood with her back to the bed and let herself fall onto it. What did she have? No ideas for a new book. A bungled photograph assignment. An absentee husband.

And Grandmama. A wave of fondness filled her chest as she thought of her faithful grandmother. At least she had always been there for her and never failed her in any way. If anything, it was Felicia who'd fallen short. She was the one who'd found pleasure in being spiteful and unruly at her grandmama's expense. The dowager wouldn't always be there for her, and Felicia suddenly had a new purpose. She sprang out of bed and readied herself for lunch.

The back garden was delightful. Boswell had green fingers. There were large batches of colourful flower beds, herbaceous borders, and wisteria growing along a fence line. The man was busy watering, weeding, and trimming old branches to make way for new growth.

"It's ham salad, madam, with fresh bread," Burton said as he brought out a tray.

"Thank you," Felicia said. Cook always served more than she could eat.

"Is there anything else, madam?" Burton asked.

"Would you send Daphne to Hartigan House with a message for the dowager Lady Gold, enquiring if she'd be available for a visit tomorrow morning?"

"Yes, madam."

Felicia finished her salad and pondered what she should do with the rest of her afternoon. Should she take her camera out again and see if she could spot any interesting subjects to photograph? Or her latest, unfinished mystery novel was still awaiting her attention. Perhaps a new hobby was in order. Many ladies enjoyed painting.

Felicia was halfway up the staircase when she heard the front door open, and two male voices reached her. Charles was home! She pivoted and headed back down, and whilst still hidden by the curve in the staircase, overheard Charles say to Burton, "I need you to keep a careful eye on her."

Felicia froze. Charles could only be referring to her, but why would he ask his butler to keep an eye on her? Had he given similar instructions in the past? That would explain why she often felt Burton hovering in a manner that made her uncomfortable.

The conversation stopped, and Felicia continued her descent down the stairs. "Hello, love," she said when Charles spotted her.

He seemed startled to see her so soon after Burton had walked away but recovered with a broad smile. "Felicia, darling."

"You're home."

"Well, yes. I live here."

Felicia was pleased to see him and didn't want to start an argument or make whatever time Charles had for her disagreeable. She embraced him and greeted him with a kiss.

"Are you hungry?" she asked. "I've just had lunch but don't mind sitting with you whilst you eat."

"I've eaten, but a cup of tea would be nice." Charles nodded. "In the drawing room? I've got something I want to ask you."

So that was why he was home. He needed information. Felicia pushed down feelings of disgruntlement. They really were uncalled for. It was natural for a husband and wife to converse and ask questions of each other.

Charles took her hand as they headed for the drawing room, and once there, Felicia rang the bell for tea. Charles took one of the armchairs leaving

Felicia to take the one opposite him. It gave her an excellent opportunity to look at and watch him.

And he, her, she supposed.

After a beat, Charles asked her, "How has your day been so far?"

"Fairly uneventful. I went to Mayfair and did a bit of shopping." Felicia glossed over her time at Lady Gold Investigations by adding, "I called in to see Ginger, but she was busy. In fact, she commissioned me to bring Boss back to Hartigan House."

Charles laughed. "Is that so?"

Felicia reciprocated the question. "How has your day been?"

"Also uneventful," Charles said.

Felicia considered her husband, the intelligence behind his eyes, his easy-going manner, his confidence, and how handsome she'd found him when they'd first met. How handsome she still found him. She'd been delighted when he'd begun to court her and blissfully happy when they'd wed. She'd imagined them spending hours every day in the marriage bed, and if not there, strolling arm in arm throughout London, staring at each other with stars in their eyes as lovers do.

It hadn't turned out that way. Certainly, the first few weeks had been bliss, but then Charles became busier with whatever he did at the House of Lords every day, and after a short hope for motherhood that was dashed, Felicia felt her light slowly dimming. The man who sat across from her seemed a stranger.

"Felicia?" Charles snapped his fingers. "I lost you."

Felicia pushed a strand of her dark bob behind her ear. "Oh, I'm so sorry."

"That's all right," he said. "The recounting of my day would put anyone to sleep."

Daphne arrived with the tea, then left them alone again. Felicia poured and handed Charles his cup and saucer before returning to her seat.

After the ritual of blowing and sipping, Charles said, "Why didn't you tell me about the notes?"

So that's the reason he's come home early.

"Who told you about the notes? Ginger?" Felicia felt an unreasonable sense of betrayal.

"Don't be angry. She's worried about you, love." Charles stroked her arm. "I don't understand why you didn't show them to me."

Felicia bristled. After all, Charles kept things from her. "I didn't think they were important. Just a ne'er-do-well getting a cheap thrill."

"But what if it's more than that?"

Felicia inclined her head. "Like what?"

Charles shrugged. "Who's to say? One can't

predict how a mentally unhinged person will act. Perhaps someone is spying on us. On you."

Spying.

The word jumped out at her. It wasn't the first time the thought of espionage in relation to her husband had crossed her mind. Charles was inordinately busy for a man of his station. He was secretive, and sly, often distracted, and there were times, if Felicia hadn't known better, that she would have wondered if he had another family somewhere.

Of course, both ideas were preposterous.

Weren't they?

"All right," Felicia said. "I'll show you the notes, but I'll have to get them back from Ginger."

"Can you remember what they say? You can just tell me."

"The writer seems to think that he or she knows something about my past that I apparently don't know. It's all rubbish."

"Like what?" Charles pressed. "Ginger seemed to think the Duke of Worthington was implicated somehow."

"Why yes, but that's too outrageous to consider. I have nothing to do with the man. The writer of these annoying notes obviously knew about the duke planning to wed, and that event was top of their mind as he or she typed."

Charles sipped his tea, keeping his eyes on her the whole time. After placing his cup and saucer on the small table at his elbow, he said, "All the same, I'd like you to be particularly careful, especially whilst the gunman is at large."

"The gunman who shot Hazel Wright?" Felicia nearly scoffed, but seeing the seriousness of Charles' expression, she nodded instead. "Of course."

Charles got to his feet and extended a hand to Felicia. She accepted and sighed into Charles' chest as he embraced her. Yes, she loved this man, and he loved her. They would be all right.

"Shall we make plans for dinner?" she asked, looking up at him.

Something flashed behind Charles' eyes. The darkness of regret. "I'm afraid I'm needed elsewhere tonight. But another evening for certain."

Felicia watched as Charles left, her joy gone. Its disappearance was no longer the soft hiss of a balloon slowly losing air but a loud, startling bang as it burst.

CHAPTER SIXTEEN

The next morning unfolded as mornings usually did: Ginger rose early to feed Rosa, Basil popped in to play with her, and then they met in the morning room for breakfast. Basil headed to his office at Scotland Yard and Ginger to her study at the back of the house. At some point, she met with Mrs. Beasley to plan the meals for the day or week, and then, if need be, she would go into either her office at Feathers & Flair or Lady Gold Investigations and sometimes both.

She was seated at her desk, formerly her father's desk, which had a decidedly masculine feel. The desk was a large, heavy wooden structure with ornate trim around the edges of the top and on the legs. Her desk faced a stone fireplace, and a stocked bookshelf took up most of the wall along the window.

Ginger opened the last envelope that had come to her in the post, from a supplier of fabric from the Continent announcing new designs, and she put it in the pile of things to attend to for her dress shop. She was interrupted by a knock on the door. It was cracked open, and she saw her butler standing on the other side.

"Come in, Digby," she said lightly.

Shorter and more rotund than Pippins, Digby stepped inside and held out a silver salver. On it was a single envelope. "This came by messenger, madam."

Ginger accepted the envelope, which had only her name, Mrs. Basil Reed, neatly written on the front, and no indication as to who it was from. "Thank you, Digby," Ginger said with a nod. The butler recognised his dismissal and left her alone with the mystery letter.

Opening it, Ginger sucked in a breath of surprise. The short missive was from the Duke of Worthington and was written on thick paper with the ducal crest at the top.

Dear Mrs. Reed,

> *I hope this letter finds you well. Please forgive me for*

getting right to the point, but I fear there's no time for pleasantries under the circumstances.

As you know, my beautiful Hazel has been taken from me most viciously. Of course, I recall the part you played in solving the murder of my brother and his wife, and I am asking you, most humbly, if you'd be willing to work on this case for me. It's not that I don't have confidence in the police, but I know they are busy and distracted, and unfortunately, my Hazel isn't the only murder under investigation. I want to employ someone with experience and positive results to focus solely on my Hazel's death and to track down her killer. I would most appreciate it if that person was you.

If you are willing, please contact me at my residence.
Yours most sincerely,
Worthington

Ginger let the letter fall on her desk as her gaze went to the ceiling. What an interesting turn of events.

Grabbing her things, she let Digby know she'd be stepping out. The butler simply nodded as this was a normal occurrence.

"Where should I say you are should someone enquire, madam?"

Ginger knew Digby was asking which office

she'd be at and wasn't being nosy. "Nowhere specific," she said. "I've got errands to run."

She allowed Marvin the pleasure of backing her Crossley out of the garage, then motored down the back lane toward Belgravia.

CHAPTER SEVENTEEN

The duke lived in one of the desirable residences on Eaton Square. Ginger told the butler she was there to see the duke at his invitation.

"The duke is expecting you," the butler said. "Please follow me."

The butler, as expected, led Ginger to a lovely sitting room decorated in the latest *art décoratif* style. Ginger admired the room and couldn't help but feel surprised that the older man had kept up with interior design trends. Perhaps that had been the influence of Miss Wright, who'd expected to be mistress of the place.

The Duke of Worthington stood when he saw Ginger. He seemed to have aged since the wedding day—his stoop more pronounced, making him look shorter. The skin on his face was paler, hanging loosely from apparent weight loss. The poor man looked like he needed a good meal and a long sleep.

Ginger approached and reached out her gloved hand. "Your Grace. Again, I extend my condolences. I hope you are holding up all right."

"Thank you, Mrs. Reed. I'm doing as well as can be expected." The duke waved to a captain's chair, wood-trimmed with a semi-circular frame that made up the back and side and upholstered in green with a gold geometrical pattern. Ginger gazed at it with admiration before sitting. "Can I offer you something to eat? Polly has brought tea, but if you'd prefer coffee or something else, please allow me to order it."

"Tea is fine, Your Grace, thank you, and I've recently eaten." Ginger was eager to speak about the case, and ordering food and drink would prolong things. She poured for the duke and herself, then said, "We should talk about your request."

"Indeed," the duke agreed with a sigh. "I still can't believe my Hazel is gone."

"Can one assume it wasn't a classic case of love at first sight?" Ginger asked.

"Well, for me it was." The duke's lips pulled into a smile as he remembered. "I was at an autumn dance—I may have mentioned this already—and spotted Hazel across the room. She was the most beautiful creature I'd seen in a long time." He glanced at Ginger. "You've seen her. A belligerent and entitled youth was accosting her, and something in me burst into flames. Foolishness, now when I recall it, but I strutted over like a knight about to rescue his fair maiden and scared that young buck away. Hazel's eyes twinkled as she stared up at me. My pride likes to think her look was of amazement and admiration. She said, 'Thank you, kind sir.'

"I introduced myself, and you'll forgive me, used my standing as a duke to its utmost potential. And it worked. Hazel linked her arm in mine and remained my companion for the rest of the evening. We've hardly been parted since that day."

The duke glanced away as he swallowed hard, and Ginger's heart hurt for the man. He clearly loved Miss Wright, and she couldn't believe he'd have had anything to do with her death, especially not in one that had occurred in such a spectacular way. He'd have hoped and dreamed of finishing his days on the earth with a lovely bride at his side, and now he was alone.

It did bring up one question. "Forgive me for pointing out, Your Grace, that you've gone many years, decades, as one of the most eligible bachelors in England. What compelled you to go to the altar this time?"

The duke shrugged. "My age, I suppose. I have no heirs, and Hazel was my last opportunity to rectify that." He coughed into his hand, then continued. "So, to the reason I asked you to come: the murderer must be found and brought to justice."

Ginger couldn't have agreed more. "The police are doing their best."

The duke raised a white brow. "Are they? Do they have a list of suspects? Have they found the murder weapon?"

Ginger didn't know the answer to any of those questions.

The duke leaned forward. "I know this is asking a lot of you, but I believe you have a way of finding information, *extracting* information if you will, that a man with the look of the police cannot do. Your husband is doing what the police can. Will you do what a lady can? Find the truth so that your husband can make the arrest?"

Because of Ginger's connection with Ambrosia and Felicia, she knew she should say no, stay out of it and let the law work itself out. But Felicia was in danger, Ginger was certain of that, and the duke did have a point. Ginger was a good sleuth.

"All right," she heard herself say. "I can't promise anything, but I'll take your case, Your Grace."

For the first time, the duke's shoulders relaxed. "Jolly good, Mrs. Reed. Jolly good."

A memory flashed in Ginger's mind. "You are acquainted with Lady Eliza Banks, aren't you, Your Grace?"

"I am." The duke stared back with a look of confusion. "Why do you ask?"

"It's probably nothing, but I noticed her at your pre-wedding dinner and that she looked rather unhappy. Angry even."

The duke sighed. "I'm afraid I may have inadvertently misled her about my intentions. Lady Eliza and I had kept company, and I think she was rather hopeful. But then I met Hazel."

"I see." A woman scorned, then? Could Lady Eliza be behind the shooting?

Ginger rose and offered her hand. "I'll keep in touch, Your Grace. Do try to get some rest."

LADY ELIZA HAD the look of passing beauty. She had blue eyes, too icy to seem soft, blond hair that had hints of grey, and fine lines were worked between her eyebrows and above her upper lip, quite likely from her habit of pursing her lips. The piercing envy in the lady's eyes that Ginger had witnessed at the pre-wedding dinner was gone, replaced with nervousness and unease.

"I agreed to see you only because I'd been informed that you were once Lady Gold."

"That is true," Ginger said. "My first husband was Daniel, Lord Gold. His grandmother is still alive, the dowager Lady Gold."

"You must be here on account of Miss Wright's unfortunate demise. I gather in your role as a lady investigator."

Lady Eliza said the words "lady investigator" in the same tone one would describe a taste of bad fish.

"I am, in fact," Ginger admitted. "His Grace, the Duke of Worthington, has asked me to make enquiries."

"And that brought you to me?" Lady Eliza said with a note of indignation.

"I'm afraid there's a feeling that you and Miss Wright hadn't got off on the right foot."

Lady Eliza huffed. "I couldn't stand the wretch."

Ginger kept her expression placid, even though the strength of the lady's words shocked her. "And why is that?"

"Pfff. She was a gold-digger, plain and simple. A pretty little thing like that had no prospects on her own. She needed to marry well to live well, and I didn't begrudge her that. But the duke? When there were plenty of other wealthy men of lower rank and closer to her age to choose from?"

"Perhaps that's true," Ginger said, "but why did it matter so much to you? The duke wouldn't have been the first man to become beguiled by a young pretty thing."

Lady Eliza's back stiffened, her chin rose. Her lips formed a tight line, and Ginger thought she spotted them quiver. Lady Eliza was fighting to remain in control of her emotions.

Suddenly, Ginger understood why. "Are you in love with the duke, Lady Eliza?"

Lady Eliza jerked, her eyes locking on Ginger's with contempt. "How dare you?"

Perhaps, when Ginger was younger—before she'd married Daniel and spent four years in France and Belgium—she would've buckled under such loathing. Still, she kept her composure, remaining unintimidated.

"Is it true?"

"What does it matter how I feel about him."

"It's motive, Lady Eliza."

Lady Eliza's jaw dropped. "Are you accusing me of murder? I was sitting in the congregation with the Earl of Somerset."

"It's quite likely the murderer hired an assassin,"

Ginger said. "Being present in the congregation won't be considered an alibi in this instance."

"Well I never!" Lady Eliza stiffened. "I think you should leave, *Mrs. Reed.*"

"If you wish," Ginger said. "However, I could help you prove your innocence. The police are looking for anyone who might have a grudge against Miss Wright, and someone is certain to drop your name. I'm afraid you didn't do a good job of hiding your negative feelings towards Miss Wright."

Lady Eliza shivered, the first sign of vulnerability. "It was clear that I didn't like Hazel Wright, Lady Gold. I know I have a sharp tongue, but I'm not a murderer. I wouldn't even know how to hire someone to do such a deed at my request."

Lady Eliza's shoulders slumped. "I feel silly now," she said, "like a schoolgirl with a crush who went after the object of her desire. I had no chance with the duke, apparently. I've loved him for years, decades, and we were friends for a while. I fear I threw myself at him one too many times, and he turned away from me. You see, too much time was allowed to pass, and I was no longer a candidate to provide an heir."

"I'll do what I can to clear your name," Ginger said. Unless, of course, evidence pointed back to the lady. "I'm sorry you've been put through this."

Lady Eliza's hard demeanour returned. "I require no pity. My maid will see you out."

"Thank you," Ginger returned. "By the way, do you use a typewriter?"

"I have one, but I rarely use it."

"Would you mind if I see it?"

Lady Eliza lifted a shoulder. "If you must." She rang for her maid and instructed her to show Ginger to the study. There, Ginger found a letter-writing desk with a roll top and another flat-topped desk with an older Royal typewriter. The black machine had a higher back than newer models and round, metal-framed wooden keys spaced relatively far apart.

"Might I add a sheet of paper?"

"I can insert it for you, madam," the maid said, hurrying to perform the task.

Ginger typed the words 'dark back'. No misalignment was present.

Ginger's next stop was Scotland Yard.

She found Basil in his office, a humble room containing only a desk, two chairs, and a filing cabinet.

Basil looked up with mild curiosity. "Ginger?"

"Hello, love," Ginger said, taking the empty chair.

"Forgive me for dropping in unannounced, but I have news."

Basil stacked the paperwork on his desk and moved it to the side. "I'm all ears."

"The Duke of Worthington has hired me to look into the murder of Hazel Wright."

Basil frowned, his handsome hazel eyes narrowing. "The police are already investigating."

"The duke knows that and assumes we'll work together." Ginger crossed her ankles and smoothed her skirt. "He was impressed with how we solved the murders of his brother and sister-in-law. Apparently, he wants all hands on deck."

Basil leaned back in his chair and wove his fingers together. "I see. Have you made any progress?"

"I've just come from seeing the duke. I was hoping you'd have something to share with me to get me started. Any suspects?"

With a sigh, Basil said, "The cathedral was filled, and with everyone looking intently at the bride and groom, no one seems to have noticed anything amiss. Farley has been cleared."

"The duke did confirm one possible enemy," Ginger said. "Lady Eliza Banks had believed the duke had shown romantic interest in her."

Basil leaned forward. "A jealous lover?"

"I spoke to her before coming here. She denies it, of course."

"I'll take a look at her finances," Basil said. "Perhaps an unusual payment has been made, potentially to the killer."

"Have you learned anything new about Miss Wright?"

Basil huffed. "Miss Wright appears to be a ghost. Even though the duke's people had done their due diligence by thoroughly investigating Miss Wright's background, police scrutiny found no official record of her or any family or relational connections, dead or alive."

"Do you believe she was in Britain under false pretences?"

"It's a natural conclusion. The question is, why?"

Ginger's thoughts went to the Soviet club. Did Charles' visit there have anything to do with Hazel Wright?

Ginger rose to her feet. "I'll have Magna do a bit of digging."

Basil walked around the desk to her. "I would like to know how Miss Jones gets her information. Or perhaps I wouldn't. It's certainly good to have Miss Jones on your side. I'd hate to make an enemy out of the likes of her."

Ginger laughed. "She's not as scary as she looks. She's still scary, just—"

Basil cut her off with a kiss. "Just be careful, love. We can't forget that a lady died at the hands of a sniper. Nowhere is safe."

They turned at the sound of knuckles tapping on the door where Constable Braxton appeared. "Excuse me, sir," he said. "There's news from Dr. Wood. The autopsy for Miss Wright is complete."

"Very good," Basil said as he got to his feet. He looked at Ginger. "Shall we?"

Ginger had frequented many mortuaries in London, and they all had similar features. In the basement of a hospital were small high windows, if any, white porcelain sinks, and an operating table illuminated by new electric lighting that produced brighter light than the old gas or oil lamps once in use. A pungent odour of strong cleaning products mixed with the lingering scent of decay. Ginger wrapped her arms around herself in defence against the necessary cool temperature.

The mortuary where they found Dr. Wood was no different from any other. The body on the table covered in a white sheet was Miss Hazel Wright.

"Good day, Dr. Wood," Basil said. After offering further greetings, Basil asked, "Do you have news to report?"

"Indeed I do." Dr. Wood was paler than most British men due to the amount of time he spent in the hospital basement. Ginger wondered if the only time the man saw the sun was when called to an out-of-doors crime scene and was lucky enough for the clouds to part whilst he was there.

"The bullet became lodged in her neck," Dr. Wood continued, "killing her instantly."

"Can we see the bullet?" Ginger asked. No casing had been found, which wasn't unexpected, as everyone suspected the gunman was well versed in his task and wouldn't have left evidence behind.

Dr. Wood presented a small tray with the bullet on it, cleaned of blood and human tissue. "I assumed you'd want to see it before I have it delivered to the police."

Basil accepted the tray, his hazel eyes narrowing as he examined the bullet. "A .303 calibre. It's from a Short Magazine Lee-Enfield Mark III rifle."

"A standard weapon used by the British in the Great War." Ginger took the tray from Basil and examined the bullet.

"Weapons were supposed to be returned to the Crown," Basil replied. "But as we know, many 'lost' pistols and rifles were declared."

"I think we must be looking at a wedding interloper," Ginger offered.

"I agree," Basil returned. "Everyone on the guest list has been accounted for; each guest had plenty of other people to witness that they were in their seats in the nave at the time of the shooting."

Ginger returned the tray with the bullet to Dr. Wood. "How does one find a hired assassin?"

Basil groaned. "Or a needle in a haystack?"

FELICIA HAD a bit of a skip in her step as she walked across the cul-de-sac to visit her grand-mama. Charles had come home early the night before with flowers and an apology for spending so much time away. He explained that he was busy helping the police with the Hazel Wright case—everyone was a bundle of nerves—but once the killer was apprehended, he promised to spend more time with her. How he helped the police, Felicia didn't understand, but she decided to take him at his word.

Digby answered the front door—now that Felicia no longer lived at Hartigan House, she didn't feel it was proper to let herself in—and led her to the drawing room where her grandmama waited.

"Don't get up," Felicia said as she entered. Her grandmama was dressed in a high-collared lacy blouse reminiscent of the Victorian days she cherished. Felicia leaned down and kissed the matriarch's cheek. "So nice to see you, Grandmama."

"Your request for a visit was a lovely surprise," Grandmama said. "I'm usually the one to ask you."

The statement was curt but not incorrect. Felicia tried to lighten the mood. "I'm delighted it was a good time to come."

Grandmama waved bejewelled fingers—her grandmother did love her jewellery. "Is Charles at home? How is he?"

"He's fine, but not here. He's busy assisting the police with that terrible murder, the bride of the Duke of Worthington."

Grandmama's hand quivered, rattling her teacup, and Felicia feared she was about to drop it. "Grandmama?"

"It's nothing." Grandmama put her teacup on the table beside her and folded her hands on her lap. Sitting stiffly upright, she lowered her chin, the soft folds of her cheeks deepening, and stared with her large, round eyes. "What can Charles possibly do to help with that?"

Felicia shook her head. "I've wondered that myself. It is such a dreadful situation with very few leads. I suppose the police are looking for help wherever they might find it. But let's speak of happier subjects, shall we?"

"Certainly," Grandmama said. "How is the weather? I've yet to step outside."

"Or look out of the window?" Felicia asked lightly. "It's fair. Not as much sunshine as yesterday, and the breeze is cool. Are you still playing cards with Mrs. Schofield?"

"Yes," Grandmama said, "but she's a cheat. And a gossip."

Felicia held back her smile. Grandmama's widowed neighbour might have been a cheat and a gossip, but that didn't keep her grandmother from spending time with the elderly lady. Felicia suspected that Grandmama counted on the gossip to keep her abreast of the news, at least what was new in the world of high society, as Ginger never volunteered any news, a trait that Grandmama had complained to Felicia about on more than one occasion.

Felicia picked up a triangular egg and watercress sandwich and took a nibble. "Grandmama?"

"Yes, dear."

"Would you tell me about my mama and papa?" Felicia wasn't so naïve as to think her grandmama would live forever, and there were certain burning questions she had that really couldn't be left much longer.

Grandmama's large eyes blinked. "What do you want to know?"

"Anything, really. I was so young when they died. I feel like they never really existed at all."

"They certainly did exist," Grandmama said, her demeanour softening. "Your father was an easy child to bring up—" She glanced at Felicia, who smirked back. It wasn't necessary to voice that Felicia had been a difficult child; Felicia realised that now. But for the first time, she understood that she'd been Ambrosia's problem when, in a perfect world, she would've been under the instruction of her own mother and father. She wrestled with how to present an apology, but her grandmama released her by continuing.

"Your father took an interest in art and poetry, though a little attention paid to economics wouldn't have hurt. He had friends who liked to go fox hunting, and he would go with them, but I could tell he didn't like it. He was always down in the mouth the next day when recounting the story to his father."

"And Mama?"

Grandmama worked her lips. "I'm afraid I didn't approve of your mother at first, but she turned out to be a good wife for your father."

"Why didn't you approve?"

"She came from an impoverished family. I'm not

convinced it didn't contribute to our financial demise."

Felicia had become aware, after the fact, that the Gold family had been under financial hardship. It was why Daniel had left her to go to America to marry Ginger and tap into the Hartigan money. It was the only reason Bray Manor had been kept from being repossessed by the bank. Felicia had only been a child then and didn't feel any financial distress. Grandmama had kept that from her. She only remembered being irrationally angry at Daniel for leaving her—and was quite outraged when he'd returned with a wife.

"What did cause our demise, ultimately?"

"Oh, Felicia." Grandmama huffed with indignation. "Is this why you asked to visit me?"

"I have a right to know, don't I? It's natural for one to be curious about one's parents and grandparents. If you don't tell me these stories, who will?"

"My husband, Artie, was a good man but had a gambling weakness. It brought him great shame and shamed the rest of us too. I didn't understand the depths of his indebtedness until after he passed away. If it weren't for Daniel . . . and Ginger . . . we would be paupers right now, and you'd probably not be the wife of an earl. Now, I'm rather tired. Perhaps we can talk again another day." Grandmama rang for Langley and started to leave the drawing room.

Clearly, her questions had upset her grandmother, but Felicia didn't regret asking them. She understood more now why Grandmama was so pernickety. Still, Felicia felt there was more to the story, especially after Ambrosia's dramatic exit.

CHAPTER NINETEEN

Ginger met Charles at Duck Island Cottage at St. James's Park the next day. Having invited him and Felicia for dinner the night before, she could discreetly pass a message to him, which he'd acknowledged with a barely perceptible nod. The covert transaction had given Ginger a thrill, reminding her of her days working as an agent when she was often disguised or using a false identity. She had to remind herself that there had been plenty of fear attached as well, but the daring missions got her heart pumping in a way that peacetime couldn't match.

Ginger had had a brief encounter with Charles in France. He'd been working under an alias, complete with disguise, so when they met again years later in Brighton, Ginger hardly recognised him. It didn't take long before they both knew that the other had also made a vow of secrecy to the British government and never brought it up, though the undercurrent between them remained.

She parked the Crossley, then walked to the quaint cottage at the entrance of Duck Island on St. James's Park Lake. King Charles II had been a bird watcher and commissioned the aviary's development. Ginger was delighted to watch a heron soar by, its long body stretched from head to toe. Turning away from a swan that had caught her eye, Ginger headed for the bench and found that Charles had already arrived and was seated there.

"Charles," she said quietly before taking a seat. "I'm assuming all the effort means you have good information."

Charles tipped his hat, then said, "Miss Wright isn't who she claimed to be."

"Let me guess," Ginger said with a sly grin. "She's Russian."

Charles' jaw dropped. "I'm not even going to ask how you came to that conclusion, but I do think it's a shame that you're no longer active in the field."

"Yes, well, my life has changed, as have my priorities," Ginger said. "I'm doing my bit as a private citizen, doing what I can to help bring justice to those who can no longer speak for themselves."

"Yes, when you're not employed by disgruntled wives who want you to spy on their unfaithful husbands."

"Every true mission needs a cover distracting from it."

"Quite," Charles agreed.

"Do you have a name for our Russian mystery woman?"

"Irina Kuznetsova, agent of the Soviet Union."

Ginger whistled. "Soviet agents are alive and well in Britain. I suppose that's understandable. Industrialisation in the Soviet Union is growing rapidly, and Europe has taken notice."

"Yet, the Soviet Union is still recovering from the Great War. They suffered greatly and aren't a military threat. However, we mustn't let our guard down. Germany is also a wounded bear. I fear the time of peace we are now enjoying could be short-lived."

"Oh, say it isn't so, Charles. I couldn't bear another war. No one could. The Great War was the war to end all wars."

"There are those on the Continent who don't seem to have heard that," Charles said soberly. "However, perhaps I'm being too morose. I've seen and heard too many bloody disturbing things, as have you, to have faith in the ongoing goodness of mankind. But I digress. What we know is that a Soviet spy had convinced a British duke to marry and someone shot her before the vows could be spoken and certified."

"Another British agent?" Ginger said, pushing red hair off her cheek. "That would make the most sense. Clearly, it wasn't you, as you were seated in the same row as I was at the time of the shooting."

"If that is the case, it wasn't authorised. Miss Kuznetsova would've been more interesting to us alive than dead."

"Then another Soviet agent did the deed," Ginger said. "Perhaps Miss Kuznetsova's devotion to the Soviet Union had come into question. It would explain making a spectacle at the cathedral like that."

"Indeed," Charles said. "If the British were responsible, they would've arranged a motor car crash, an accidental poisoning, or something like that. Keep it out of the public eye as much as possible."

Ginger concurred with Charles' statement. "What is to be done now? Are the police chasing their tails?"

"The service would like to find the culprit responsible for this crime, especially if it's a Soviet agent."

"And if the killer is rogue?"

Charles huffed. "Even more so."

"I think we need to bring Basil into this," Ginger said. "We need the police's cooperation, and not telling them about Irina Kuznetsova is handcuffing them during their investigation."

After a long exhale, Charles said, "Perhaps you're right. You may inform him, but you can't tell him you got the information from me. No one must suspect me to be anything more than a devoted lord sitting in the House of Lords."

Ginger chortled. "Do you think you're deceiving Felicia? She might not know the truth about you, but she knows something's amiss. You mustn't underestimate her."

"Believe me, Ginger. I'm aware of that."

Ginger's next stop was Scotland Yard. She simply wiggled her fingers at the clerks and officers and giggled a greeting. "Good morning, gentlemen. I was in the area . . ."

She dropped her subterfuge when the men were behind her and out of sight. Since no one had gone out of their way to let her know that Basil was out, she assumed he was in and found her assumption correct.

"Hello, Basil."

The front desk officers weren't the only ones to

show surprise. Basil's hazel eyes widened in question. "Ginger? Has something happened?"

"Well, not exactly." Ginger closed the door behind her and took the empty chair. "But I do have information."

From his side of the desk, Basil leaned in. "All right."

"I can't reveal my source, but I ask that you trust me that it's sound."

Basil's jaw tightened. "I'll agree to that for now."

"Miss Wright was a Russian spy. Her real name is Miss Kuznetsova."

Basil's lips twitched. "Did Miss Jones tell you that?"

"As I've mentioned, I can't reveal my sources."

Basil tapped the end of his pencil on his desk. "I see. Do you have any proof? You know Morris is going to demand evidence."

Ginger sighed. "I can't provide that, at least not at the moment."

Basil narrowed his eyes. "Do you *have* proof?"

"No, I don't," Ginger answered honestly. She hadn't asked Charles for proof, and she didn't think he'd have given it to her if she had. "But I got the information from a reliable source."

"A reliable source?" Basil snorted. "I swear, Ginger, sometimes I think you are a secret agent. My only consolation is that you must work for the British, and if that's the case, they have a most excellent asset."

Fortunately, Basil had spoken in the present tense so that Ginger could answer honestly. "I promise you, Basil, on the life of our baby Rosa, that I am not a British agent. I simply know people."

"Who are or who were. Blast it, Ginger. Say I go with this information from *a reliable source.* What am I to do now? I still have no suspects."

"Perhaps it would help to work backwards," Ginger said. "I've no doubt the Duke of Worthington was in love with the person he knew as Hazel Wright, but what motivated Miss Kuznetsova to marry him?"

"The fact that the duke was nearly four decades her senior might mean she was after his money," Basil said. "An early death on his part would've given her considerable resources, assuming she worked her feminine wiles to have herself added to his will."

"Assuming she wasn't about to kill him on their wedding night—"

"A big assumption."

"Yes, but there would also be advantages to keeping him alive. The duke would've given her access to influential circles, perhaps figures with access to sensitive political or military information.

She'd have access to the House of Lords and what went on there and could listen in on political talk among the MPs and Lords."

Basil nodded. "It would've given her a legitimate reason to participate in valuable social engagements and to interact with influential people. Is it possible that the duke has information or intelligence of strategic interest to the Soviet Union?"

Ginger shrugged. "I suppose it's possible. He hardly seems the type, but perhaps he has something they want without being aware of it. Perhaps something he inherited from the former duke."

"The former duke was very political and involved in the military," Basil said thoughtfully, "though his focus was on Spain." He rubbed the back of his neck. "Am I to add the British government and the government of the Soviet Union as suspects now?"

"Perhaps we should keep our focus smaller," Ginger said. "What about Lady Eliza? Did you find anything of interest about her?"

Basil shook his head. "Her financial records are unremarkable."

Constable Braxton knocked on the door, which was cracked open. "Sir, I think you'll want to see this."

After Basil beckoned him to enter, he handed over a newspaper clipping. Basil smoothed it out on his desk, and Ginger could see a photograph of a man and woman, the woman being Hazel Wright, or rather, Irina Kuznetsova. "The man in that photograph is Mr. Farley from *London News Today*. He'd been stepping out with Miss Wright before she became engaged to the Duke of Worthington."

"Our man from the newspaper is a liar?" Basil said sarcastically. "Shocking."

"Who took the photograph?" Ginger said. "Does it say?"

"James Johnstone," Constable Braxton said. "Sadly, he's now deceased."

The clipping had come from the society pages, and Ginger noted the event. "A soirée in Sussex."

Basil looked at Ginger. "Fancy a drive down Fleet Street?"

CHAPTER TWENTY

Felicia had a short but disturbing thought. *Ginger and Grandmama knew something that they didn't want her to know.* That would explain the strange looks they sometimes shared in her presence. But why? She had a strong feeling that it had something to do with her. And those blasted notes! One didn't have to be Sherlock Holmes to figure out that the person penning those notes believed they knew something about Felicia that she wasn't privy to. And that somehow, that bit of information was connected with the Worthington family.

Felicia couldn't imagine what or how, but it irked her that Ginger might know something about her life and was purposely keeping it from her. On another day, in a saner moment, Felicia would never have done what she impulsively set out to do. Seeing that the coast was clear—no butler or maids to be seen—she slinked down the corridor leading to the back of the house and Ginger's study.

Like a blasted thief, she slid into Hartigan House, unseen, tip-toed to Ginger's study, and closed the door behind her. Felicia had been in the room a million times and had almost memorised the books on the shelves whilst spending time with Ginger. It was silly of her to think she'd find anything in there, but if Ginger were hiding something, she'd probably be hiding it from Basil, too, so whatever clue Felicia hoped to find wouldn't be in Ginger's bedroom. The library was too public, with Scout often using it to read or study. If Ginger had something hidden, it would be in this room.

Reluctant to comb through Ginger's desk, Felicia ran her fingers along the spines of the books on the shelves. Most of the titles had belonged to Mr. Hartigan, but Ginger had added new ones since, on topics ranging from business management to childcare.

The shelves and the books themselves had been carefully dusted, a testament to the proficiency of Ginger's household staff. Nothing looked odd or out of place. Felicia's focus darted to Ginger's desk.

"I'm almost out of typewriter tape," she whispered. "Ginger might have extra, and I know she wouldn't mind my borrowing some until I can replace the cartridge."

It was a feeble excuse, and had it been true, Felicia's heart wouldn't have been beating as rapidly as it was. She sat in the office chair, leaning back with her hand on her collar. Should someone come in, Ginger herself, she'd say she wanted to use the telephone. To call whom? Felicia bit her lip. Her hairdresser? No, not urgent enough. Banker? She needed to be ready with a viable excuse. Perhaps she was being silly and overreacting. She couldn't think of a believable reason she wouldn't go home and use her own telephone. It was best she did what she intended to and then leave.

Nothing of note was found in the desk drawers, but Felicia knew Ginger well enough to know that she might have a secret compartment somewhere. It took a bit of jiggling to work the drawer out of its slot, and Felicia was disappointed that she found nothing out of the ordinary about the drawer. Putting the drawer aside, she then examined the vacancy in the desk, and a careful running of her fingers along the back caused the discovery of a spring. She pulled it, and a desktop section made a snapping noise. Felicia moved the typewriter out of the way, revealing the cover of a secret compartment.

Felicia's heart beat loudly in her ears. Was she really about to invade Ginger's privacy in this way? She was only doing this because she believed Ginger and Ambrosia were conspiring together about something that had to do with her, so she justified a quick peek.

The compartment had a single old-and-ratty-looking leather-bound book. Felicia turned the front cover then gasped.

BASIL HAD INSISTED on taking his Austin, so Ginger tried to relax in the passenger seat, focusing on the beauty of London. There were times when she missed Boston. Her sister and stepmother were there, and she did sometimes miss the freedoms Americans seemed to enjoy. No class systems to fuss with, vast roadways, and distances one could travel without having to slow down because one had come to yet another town only three miles after the last one. Baseball. Ginger didn't miss the snow, however. Or the cold that came with it. But she did miss her friend Haley Higgins, soon to become a doctor. Ginger certainly hoped to revisit Boston someday.

Fleet Street was a long corridor flanked with four- and five-storey buildings made of limestone or brick, some of which housed the many newspaper publishers in London. The real beauty of the street was the view of St. Paul's Cathedral's dome to the east.

Basil parked in front of the building with a placard near the door that read "London News Today."

Ginger adjusted the strap of her handbag over the shoulder of her flowing chiffon day frock and followed Basil inside. He announced them to the receptionist, asking to see Mr. Farley.

"Mr. Farley didn't come in today," the clerk said. His prominent Adam's apple bobbed as he cleared his throat. Lowering his voice, he added, "The editor's not happy about it, either. I'm only saying this because you're the police."

"Do you have an address for Mr. Farley?" Basil asked. "We'll be sure to remind him to check in, if we find him."

The clerk scribbled an address on some paper and handed it to him. "I hope he's got a good reason for not showing up or sending a message to explain himself. If he wants to keep his job, that is."

The address was a boarding house in east London.

"I'd think a man with a successful career in photography would make enough money to live in a nicer area," Ginger said. "But perhaps he's being frugal."

"There's nothing wrong with that," Basil said.

"There certainly isn't."

The front door was opened by a woman dressed in a plain day frock covered by a well-used apron.

"Good day," Basil started. "I'm Chief Inspector Basil Reed, and this is Lady Gold, a consultant with Scotland Yard. And you are?"

"Mrs. Webber, the landlady."

"We'd like to speak to Mr. Farley."

"I hope Mr. Farley's not in trouble," Mrs. Webber said. "He's the best tenant I got. Always pays on time and in full." She frowned. "But he's usually gone during the day."

"If you'll direct us to his room, we'll see if he's in."

"Second floor, the last door on the right. And if you don't need me, I need to nip to the corner shop. I'll only be ten minutes."

"If we do," Basil said, "we can wait until you return."

Residual food smells of fried kippers or boiled mutton, mixed with tobacco smoke, clung to the corridor wallpaper, which had yellowed. Ginger noted that many of the corner pieces had begun to curl.

Basil knocked and, when nothing was heard on

the other side, spoke loudly. "Mr. Farley, it's the police. Please open up."

Ginger wrinkled her nose. Despite the lingering smells in the corridor, she detected something more putrid. "It smells of death."

Basil sniffed. "Grounds for breaking in." He shot a look at Ginger's handbag. "Would you like the honours, or shall I see if my shoulder is up to knocking the door down?"

Ginger already had her fingers in her handbag, retrieving her set of lock picks. "Allow me."

The door clicked open after a couple of minutes of listening and playing with the pins and bobs inside the lock. The foul odour intensified.

"Mr. Farley?" Basil called out as they entered. The room was plainly furnished with a single sofa with no cushions, and what looked like a tea stain on one end. Empty coffee cups sat on a low table with an overflowing ashtray. A typewriter sat on another table with two chairs, one of which had been toppled over.

Mr. Farley's body lay on its side on the floor, his head severely damaged by a close-range gunshot, with bullet holes on either side of his temple.

"Oh mercy." Ginger wasn't a doctor, but she'd seen enough death to know the victim had been dead for at least a day. Her gaze darted about the room, but no pistol was left in sight.

Basil noticed the same thing. "I'll have the men search for the murder weapon."

Ginger drew Basil's attention to a photo album lying open on the coffee table. "Nearly every photograph is of Miss Wright." She flipped the pages with her gloved hands. "He clearly had an obsession."

"Perhaps he couldn't bear living without her?" Basil said.

"Or he couldn't bear seeing her with another man and then suffered from the grief of what he'd done."

Basil's focus darted about. "Any sign of a note?"

Ginger nodded at the typewriter. "There's a card in there. It's hard to see from your vantage point." She plucked the card from the cartridge, noting it was the same size and thickness as the notes Felicia had been receiving.

My apologies to whoever finds me—Mrs. Webber, probably. I'm finished with this life. Goodbye.

Ginger automatically searched for evidence of misalignment, but none was present, and unfortunately, Mr. Farley hadn't used words with the letter *k*. A quick test proved this wasn't the machine in question.

"Shall we look for a bobby to let the Yard know we have a possible murder?"

"What makes you think it's not suicide?"

Ginger pointed to the gun on the floor. "It's sitting on Mr. Farley's left side, and he fell off the chair to the left." She motioned to the table. "Everything is situated to the right of the typewriter. That glass of water, the pen, and a pad of paper."

"Of course," Basil said. He'd been too busy looking at the photo album to take proper notice. "And here," he added pointing, "he's lifting a pint with his right hand. This could very well rule him out as our murderer." He got to his feet. "I'll go and search for a bobby. Are you all right to stay here, or would you like to come?"

"I'll wait until you get back, love," Ginger said. "Then I'm going to check on Felicia."

"Very good. I'll intercept Mrs. Webber, keep her from the shock of finding her tenant indisposed, as it were."

CHAPTER TWENTY-ONE

Diary

Belonging to Miss Ambrosia Saunders

18th April 1871

"Ambrosia Jane Saunders!"

I turned to my mother, who was characteristically unimaginative in her use of my Christian names, spoken at high volume and with a clipped tongue, such as mothers of a certain class throughout the ages have been wont to do.

"Yes, Mother?" I answered innocently.

Felicia jerked, her eyes staring ahead, unblinking, as her mind grasped the significance of what she was reading. *Grandmama had penned these words*! Felicia had never known the dowager before her hair had started turning grey, and certainly not as a lady with any youthful ideologies. She could hardly picture Ambrosia as a smooth-skinned brunette with a bounce to her step, but the tone of the words scribed in this old diary was clearly from the viewpoint of inexperience.

The volume read like a captivating memoir; Felicia wasn't the only family member with writing skills, and she forgot herself as she rapidly turned the pages.

"No!"

Felicia's chest tightened as she read Ambrosia's confession, her eyes itching with angry tears. "How could she keep this from me?"

An involuntary moan reached her lips, her vision blurring. Everything she believed about herself, her history and genealogy, was a lie.

Had Daniel known?

And how was a person to prove Grandmama's claims that Grandfather Gold wasn't her papa's father?

The pain Felicia felt was deep and hard, like someone had just punched her in the stomach, and she was about to fall to the floor. Fainting wasn't a kindness about to be given to her, though, as she remained conscious, if not soundly.

If Ambrosia's words were true—and why would she lie?—then the first Duke of Worthington was her blood grandfather. That would make the current Duke of Worthington her great uncle.

Does he know? Felicia shook her head. *No, probably not.* The question was, what was she to do now?

"Felicia?"

Felicia's cheeks burned red as she faced the familiar figure. "Hello, Ginger."

GINGER FELT SOMEWHAT STUPEFIED, seeing Felicia seated in her office chair as if she owned it. At first glance, Felicia's barely suppressed rage surprised her, but then she saw the old leather book in her former sister-in-law's hand. Ambrosia's journal. She swallowed. "What are you doing?"

Felicia held up the old diary. "You must forgive me for snooping, but I knew you and Grandmama were keeping secrets from me. And with the mysterious notes about the Worthington connection with me, well, I betrayed your confidence to get to the truth." She raised a defensive palm. "Only because I knew I'd never get the truth out of either of you."

Ginger lowered herself onto one of the empty wood-and-leather chairs facing her desk. "I wanted to tell you."

Felicia snorted. "I know Grandmama tied your hands, of course. But after all this time, after my parents and Daniel have been gone for so long, why not tell me?"

"You mustn't be so hard on Ambrosia," Ginger said. "Rightly or wrongly, she wanted to protect you from the scandal that would surely arise if this got out."

"Did she care to protect my reputation or hers?" Felicia asked bitterly.

"Probably a bit of both," Ginger admitted. "I believe this was one of the reasons she was so eager for you to marry well. So the scandal, if it came out, wouldn't prevent you from making a good match."

Felicia scoffed. "My marriage is a sham. My husband presents himself to me but only lets me know one side. A thin side. I might as well be married to one of the characters in my own books."

"Felicia . . ."

"It's true. No lord I know of spends as much time at the House as he does. If I didn't know better, I'd think he was having an affair." She glanced at Ginger, her eyes flashing briefly with guilt. "I learned a thing or two working for you, Ginger. I'm pretty certain he's not having an affair."

"You followed him?"

"Don't look so shocked. Of course I did. With my fancy new camera at my disposal. Not one single instance alone with another woman."

"You sound disappointed."

"Not disappointed, just *aware*. An affair I could understand, even if I would despise him for it. But just routine business? He'd rather be with his cronies, or worse, alone, than with me."

"Charles loves you very much, Felicia. I can attest to that."

"Basil loves *you* very much, Ginger. He's also busy with his work, but he includes you in it. He shares his days, confides in you, and asks your opinion. That's love."

Ginger sighed. Felicia wasn't wrong. Basil was a step above most men, and Ginger was grateful to have him in her life. Basil loved her, and she loved him as deeply in return. Though . . . She pushed a wave of regret away. Like with Charles, there was a part of herself she couldn't share with Basil. And Ginger knew that Basil knew that. He'd come to peace with the fact. If only Felicia could as well, but she sounded a long way from that point at the moment.

"Charles cares for me like he cares for his horse," Felicia continued with a sniffle. "Keep me fed, brushed, and exercised so I'll perform my duties when needed."

Ginger considered Felicia, who was suffering from two wounds: one inflicted by Charles and one by Ambrosia. Ginger could do nothing about the ones from Charles, but perhaps she could bring some relief to Felicia for the one caused by Ambrosia.

"Would you like to meet the duke?"

Felicia stared back in confusion. "I've already met him."

"I mean, as his niece."

"Does *he* know?"

"No, but I don't think he'll be surprised. His brother was, uh, let's say, a bit of a heartbreaker in his youth, something the current duke witnessed firsthand."

"Oh, blast it." Felicia exhaled deeply, and Ginger hoped some pent-up anger was breathed out with it.

"I don't know," Felicia said finally. "What good could it possibly serve? Grandmama would never forgive me for announcing her 'private shame' to the world, and the duke will likely see me as a gold-digger, hoping he'll add me to his will."

"Perhaps," Ginger said. "But he is an elderly man with no family, and now with his bride gone, quite lonely, I suspect. He might appreciate a bit of family in his life, even if it is a newly presented great niece." Ginger lifted a shoulder. "Ambrosia needn't know. And I don't think the duke will want to draw attention to his brother's past."

"But why should he believe me?" Felicia asked. "If the former duke was such a rake, then there could be any number of illegitimate children around."

Ginger hummed. She knew this to be true, and it made her wonder about the letter writer. But if the author of those mystery notes were also of the Worthington bloodline, why not make a claim himself? Or herself?

Lack of proof, perhaps. But what did the writer hope to achieve by sending the notes to Felicia? Did he or she hope Felicia would make a claim? Then what?

"I would like to meet the duke as my uncle," Felicia said, "but Grandmama would need to do it with me. The duke wouldn't doubt her word. There are facts in her diary that would prove to the duke that she was with his brother at a time that would line up with my father's birth."

Ginger whistled. "You have your work cut out for you, Felicia. Ambrosia is a tough nut to crack."

"That's true. But I'm all the family she has, and if she ever wants me to speak to her again, she'd better start talking." Felicia grabbed the diary, pushed away from the desk, and stormed out of the room.

Ginger remained seated, feeling like a hurricane force had just pinned her to her chair. She debated swiftly: should she go after Felicia? It wasn't as if

Felicia would harm her grandmother, at least not physically. However, Felicia's tongue could cut just as sharply as Ambrosia's, and left alone, they might slice each other to pieces.

Ginger sprang to her feet. "Felicia!"

CHAPTER TWENTY-TWO

"Grandmama!"

Ginger hurried to keep up with Felicia, who'd already reached the staircase. Digby, who'd been coming down, pushed himself against the opposite rail. From her position on the top landing, poor Lizzie, with bedlinen stacked in her arms, spotted the furious Felicia energetically climbing the stairs and wisely scampered away.

"Grandmama!"

"Felicia, love," Ginger said from behind, having caught up. "You're frightening the staff."

"She wasn't in the sitting room or the drawing room. She must be in her bedroom."

"And likely having an afternoon nap." Ginger gripped Felicia's arm when they reached the top. "I beseech you to take a breath and think about what you're doing."

Felicia did as Ginger asked, pausing long enough to breathe deeply, closing her eyes as she did so, but was undeterred. "I promise to manage my emotions, but I won't pretend I don't know."

Felicia knocked on Ambrosia's door, which Ambrosia's maid Langley answered. "I need a few moments of privacy with her ladyship."

Langley's gaze went to her mistress, and Ambrosia nodded, releasing her to go. "Is the house on fire? It's a good thing I'm not sleeping in my bed. You caught me letter writing."

Felicia raised the diary into the air. "Writing to the Duke of Worthington, perhaps?"

Ambrosia turned sharply to stare at Ginger, her large round eyes narrowing to slits. "Georgia! I trusted you."

"You mustn't blame Ginger," Felicia said. "I found this myself, shamelessly snooping. It'd become clear to me, with the mystery notes, that something was amiss and that the two of you seemed to be privy to information I was not. Information that clearly affects me."

Sitting stiff and straight, Ambrosia, her bony hand adorned with impressive rings and resting on the silver handle of her walking stick, considered

Felicia coolly. "It in no way affects you. You've eaten from the tree of knowledge and, consequently, you're suffering the emotional effects of that, but in every practical way, nothing changes for you."

"I beg to differ, Grandmama. I've gone from having one blood relative on this earth, you, to two. I desire to become acquainted with my great uncle whilst there's still time."

"That is utter poppycock!"

"Grandmother . . ." Ginger started.

Ambrosia silenced her with a look. "Apart from the fact that you carelessly stored property that belongs to me, you have nothing to do with this." She held out her hand, blue veins protruding from pale, thin skin, her palm quivering slightly. "Give that back to me, Felicia."

Felicia held on to the volume. "Not until you agree to come with me to visit the duke and verify my claim."

Ambrosia huffed. "You're making a claim to his fortune? Surely you have enough money with my inheritance that will come to you, and that of Charles. You hardly have to worry about becoming a pauper."

"I have no financial claim, Grandmama. I know that full well. My claim is relational."

Ambrosia banged her walking stick on the floor

stubbornly, but obstinacy ran in the family, and Felicia simply folded her arms, the diary firmly in her grasp. "If we're ever to converse again, you'll agree."

Ambrosia made a new appeal. "Ginger, talk sense into her. If this matter was to get into the wrong hands—and these kinds of things always do—it could destroy her."

Ginger lifted a shoulder. "She has a point, Felicia. You will become the news of the week on the society pages. Photographers will be dogging you."

"But I'll have the duke," Felicia pouted. "I'll have the truth."

Felicia changed her posture, stepping towards Ambrosia with the diary extended. "No one need know. Just you, me, Ginger, and the duke."

"What makes you think you can trust *him*?" Ambrosia asked, snatching the diary. She held it close to her chest. "One brother can be as bad as the next."

"Or the opposite," Ginger said. "I believe in this duke's character. He's truly broken up over the loss of Miss Wright. I can vouch for that."

Ambrosia stuck her chin in the air. "It's two against one, so I'm defeated. I can't go through the rest of my life with Felicia refusing to talk to me. I just don't have the strength for it."

"Thank you, Grandmama," Felicia said with apparent relief. "Thank you."

"If my life makes it into the society pages as the scandal *du jour*," Ambrosia said, vying for the last word, "I'll probably die from embarrassment anyway."

The next morning, the Duke of Worthington arrived at Hartigan House for coffee. Ginger stood behind Digby as he opened the door. The duke's skin was ashen and seemed to hang more loosely on his face. He removed his black hat as he stepped inside, holding it in front of his black suit, his very stance proclaiming his deep sorrow.

Ginger offered her hand.

"Your Grace. Thank you for coming. I know this is a difficult time."

"You did me a favour by giving me a reason to leave my house, Mrs. Reed."

Ginger linked her arm with the elderly duke's as a gracious gesture and because the duke didn't look that sure-footed. He'd come with his driver, who'd been guided to the staff quarters by Digby.

"Your message indicated that you had news," the duke said. "Is there a break in the case?"

"Not exactly." Ginger paused outside of the drawing room doors. "Though, what I do have to tell you might give you a bit of a shock."

"Oh dear," the duke said. "I suppose I should be sitting down then."

Ginger opened the doors and led the duke inside, where Ambrosia and Felicia were waiting. The coffee had already been delivered and was sitting on the low table in front of the empty settee. Felicia and Ambrosia each occupied one of the matching armchairs. Ambrosia looked like a figure created at Madame Tussaud's Wax Museum—pale and waxy. Felicia had the wide-eyed look of a young woman who suddenly found herself in the presence of a film star.

Ginger presented the duke. "Your Grace, may I present the dowager Lady Gold, whom you've met, and her granddaughter, Lady Davenport-Witt."

The duke bowed politely before taking each lady's gloved hand. "It's a pleasure."

After Ginger motioned to the settee, she and the duke took a seat. Ginger poured out four cups of coffee.

The duke's eyes, small beneath folds of skin, flashed with curiosity as he accepted the cup.

Ginger filled the silence by saying, "Lady Gold is the grandmother of my first husband, the late Lord Daniel Gold. She lives with me. Felicia is Daniel's sister. To my great pleasure, she and her husband, the Earl of Witt, have taken up residence across the street."

"We offer our condolences on your recent loss," Ambrosia said, speaking for Felicia, who was uncharacteristically mute, and offered a nod.

"Thank you, Lady Gold, Lady Davenport-Witt." The duke eyed both of the Gold ladies. "Forgive me, but I feel like we've met, though I'm afraid my old mind isn't what it used to be."

Finding her tongue, Felicia blurted, "I was at your pre-wedding reception at the Ritz with Mrs. Reed. Perhaps you saw me there. I was also at the wedding when . . . well, I'm certain you didn't see me in that sea of faces."

"Ah," the duke said, then sipped his coffee.

Ginger shot a look at Ambrosia as if to say, *Now would be a good time.*

As if to gird herself, Ambrosia inhaled. "We were acquainted many years ago, Your Grace. Many, many years ago."

The duke cocked his head, staring as if his mind was searching for answers to the clue. And then, as if hit with a memory, said, "Miss Saunders?"

Ambrosia jerked. "You remember me?"

The duke chuckled. "They say the long-term memories are the last to go." His countenance darkened. "You were friends with my sister-in-law Deborah."

"Yes, before she married your brother."

"I'm not privy to the ins and outs of a group of young ladies, but it did appear that there was a falling out between friends. There was talk about it at the time."

Ambrosia gave a quick nod. "That's true."

"Actually, that story is part of why I've invited you here, Your Grace," Ginger said. "Along with Lady Gold and Lady Davenport-Witt."

"I'm all ears," the duke said, leaning in. "I'll admit my curiosity is greatly piqued."

Ginger looked at Ambrosia and prompted, "Grandmother?"

Ambrosia sipped her coffee, then set the cup and saucer on the table at her elbow. Folding her hands in her lap, she lifted her chin. "This is a difficult admission to make, Lord Percy," she said, using his previous title. "However, I've kept the secret for as long as the fates would bear it. If it weren't for the fact that Felicia's life might be in danger, I would've taken this truth with me to the grave."

"It's obvious that what you have to say to me is causing you distress, Lady Gold," the duke said. "Please be assured that I will feel no ill will or negativity towards you, no matter the message."

Ambrosia let out a long breath. Once fortified, she said, "My confession is that I was more than simply an acquaintance of your brother, Theodore. I was under the impression that we had an understanding. That doesn't excuse my lack of restraint. However, my poor judgement put me in the situation of being with child and unmarried."

"Theo's child?"

Ambrosia nodded. "Yes. By the time I realised, he'd proposed to Deborah. I told Artemis Gold about my predicament, and he offered to marry me. It wasn't completely altruistic on his part. My family helped him out of a dire financial crisis in return."

The duke's complexion grew waxen, before red blooms burst on his ruddy cheeks. It was clear good breeding was at work as he fought back strong emotion. He swallowed hard, then said, "I apologise on my brother's behalf."

Ambrosia lifted her soft chin. "You're very quick to believe my story."

"Forgive me for speaking ill of the dead, but he was a cad right to the end. He was a thorn in my flesh all his bombastic life, and now it seems, he still has the ability to enrage me in his death." His eyes, round and glossy with shock, moved to Felicia. He stared intently, before saying, "But perhaps, you are a silver lining, a descendent of my brother?"

"His granddaughter," Felicia said. "I'm completely stunned by this news, as you must be. My grandmother did an excellent job of hiding the truth."

Facing Ginger, the duke, having regained his composure, asked, "What kind of danger is Lady Davenport-Witt in?"

"We're not exactly certain," Ginger said. "She's been receiving nuisance notes that make it quite clear that the writer knows of her true lineage."

"And how would he know that?" the duke asked.

Ginger shook her head. "We have no idea. After what happened to Miss Wright, we feel we can't take any chances."

The duke's expression darkened. "Yes, I see."

Ginger lifted the coffee pot. "Would you like more coffee, Your Grace? Perhaps with a shot of something stronger?"

The duke stared back in appreciation. "That would be splendid."

Ginger moved to the drinks trolley in the corner and poured a small glass of brandy. Returning to her spot beside the duke, she poured it into his coffee cup.

"I wouldn't mind a bit of that myself," Ambrosia said.

"Me too," Felicia chimed in.

Ginger smiled as she returned to the drinks

trolley and poured a dollop into Ambrosia's and Felicia's cups, then as an afterthought, into her own as well.

After a sip of his enhanced coffee, the duke turned to Felicia and repeated the sentiment, "So, we're related, then."

"Yes, Your Grace," Felicia said. "I'm your great niece."

The duke hummed, his eyes on her face, then took another long sip of his coffee.

Ginger hadn't expected a warm family reunion. She'd braced herself for adamant denial on the duke's part, but he was strangely accepting of this news. He apparently had more respect for Ambrosia, whom he barely knew, than his brother, whom he'd known all too well.

Before Ginger could say anything to advance the conversation, the doors to the drawing room opened. To her surprise, Basil stepped in, his expression one of distress. She understood why when he was followed into the room by Superintendent Morris and a uniformed officer who Ginger thought looked rather sheepish even though he was simply fulfilling his duty.

"I apologise, everyone," Basil said. "I wanted to send a message ahead . . ."

"But I stopped him," Superintendent Morris blustered. "It would be imprudent to allow for an escape."

Ginger stood. "What on earth are you trying to say? Who would want to escape and why?"

The superintendent stepped towards Felicia. "Lady Davenport-Witt, I must insist you come with me to Scotland Yard."

CHAPTER TWENTY-THREE

A mild uproar erupted. Ambrosia snorted in a most unladylike manner. "This is ridiculous."

The duke stood, his palms raised. "Is it necessary to create a dramatic scene? I'm certain Lady Davenport-Witt would've come to see you if you'd simply asked."

Ginger stared at her husband. "Basil?"

Basil opened his palms. His boss was unpredictable at best and unreasonable at worst; Ginger knew this.

Superintendent Morris was unmoved.

"On what grounds are you taking the lady to Scotland Yard?" the duke asked.

"On suspicion of murder, Your Grace." Superintendent Morris smirked. "It's come to the Yard's attention that Lady Davenport-Witt had means, opportunity, and *motive*."

Ginger scowled at the man who looked like a fox who thought he'd caught a mouse.

"I'm quite aware of the apparent motive," the duke said. "I hardly think that makes the lady a murderer."

Superintendent Morris' thick shoulders slumped. Ginger wasn't surprised when he stuck out his chin—a man with as much hubris as the superintendent enjoyed having his feathers ruffled. The challenge seemed to tantalise him.

"If Lady Davenport-Witt is innocent, she has nothing to fear by coming with us to be interviewed." He turned to the young officer. "Reynolds, assist the lady."

"I'll go without assistance," Felicia said, her eyes bright with indignation. "I have nothing to hide and, therefore, nothing to fear. Ginger, could you track down Charles?"

"I've already done so," Basil said. "He promised to meet you there."

Felicia walked out with Basil and the superintendent with her head held high, and Ginger couldn't have been prouder.

Ambrosia struck the floor with her walking stick. "What utter nonsense. And whilst they're flitting about harassing a perfectly innocent and respectable lady, the real killer is out there laughing."

The duke, seated again, took the final sip of his coffee before saying, "How did that bothersome superintendent find out the truth about Lady Davenport-Witt's lineage?" He stared at Ginger and then Ambrosia. "Based on today's conversation, I assume the two of you haven't let word get out."

"You assume correctly," Ambrosia said. Her round, bulbous eyes blinked back anger. "How anyone could know is beyond me. Unless . . ." She looked at Ginger. "Felicia found my diary. Is it possible someone else might have?"

Ginger shook her head. "No, Grandmother. I had it hidden carefully."

An awkward silence descended. Sharing the news that Felicia was the duke's niece was now done. What he intended to do with the information, Ginger could only guess. Felicia would have to fight for her inheritance, and with no proof other than Ambrosia's word, the courts wouldn't likely give her any merit. The only thing a claim would do would be to drag Ambrosia's reputation through the mud and Felicia's as well.

If the duke changed his will and named Felicia as the heir, things would be righted. He could even do it without stating why, leaving a mass of speculation behind after his passing.

Only time would tell. Either way, the truth was out, and, hopefully, Felicia's reputation would be protected as a result. Even Superintendent Morris would have to come around. After all, Felicia wasn't the one putting anyone in danger—*she* was the one in harm's way. At least she was safe at Scotland Yard, even if she was there for the wrong reasons. Basil and Charles were sure to look out for her.

The duke placed a fist to his mouth and softly cleared his throat. "Perhaps you wouldn't mind ringing for my driver, Mrs. Reed."

"Of course," Ginger said as she rang the bell. "You've had more excitement than you bargained for this morning."

Digby entered, and Ginger made the duke's request, asking for Ambrosia's maid to be called for as well.

Soon the maid appeared, and Ginger walked with Ambrosia and the duke to the front entrance. Ambrosia said her polite goodbyes before Langley helped her up the staircase to her bedroom.

The duke's chauffeur handed him a scarf and gloves.

"Mrs. Reed," the duke said once they were

donned. "It's been a pleasure. You will continue with the work we agreed upon, won't you?"

"I will," Ginger said. "I'm more determined now than ever to find the culprit in light of the suspicions cast in Lady Davenport-Witt's direction."

The duke tipped his hat. "Very good. I look forward to hearing from you again soon."

Ginger watched through one of the tall windows that flanked the heavy wooden door as the duke's driver opened the door to the back seat, giving unobtrusive assistance.

"Madam?"

Ginger turned to Digby, finding him waiting in the wings. He asked, "Are you in need of anything?"

"I'm afraid I need a great many things, Digby, but alas, nothing that you can give me at the moment. However, if anyone is looking for me, you may tell them I've gone to Lady Davenport-Witt's residence." Ginger paused, then added, "She may need a few items."

The butler nodded before pivoting and walking away. Ginger let herself out of the front door and strolled purposefully across the street. Packing for Felicia had been an excuse. What Ginger really wanted to do was to have another look at the photographs Felicia had taken at the cathedral. She was grasping at straws, but she needed to do something. Superintendent Morris would most certainly not allow her to view the photographs taken by the police. He probably had looked at them, and Basil, too, and Basil hadn't found anything that would lead to the killer's identity.

Would Felicia's photographs prove to be any better? One could only hope.

CHAPTER TWENTY-FOUR

Felicia felt both terrified and intrigued. Interestingly, this wasn't the first time she'd been a murder suspect, and like the previous instance, she was sure her innocence would come to light.

Fairly sure.

Charles had greeted her in the lobby of Scotland Yard, squeezed her hand, and whispered in her ear that everything would be all right. Despite his right to be present at the interview, Superintendent Morris refused to let him come into the small, stuffy room. She was there with Basil, the obnoxious superintendent, and the Davenport-Witts' family solicitor, Mr. Neil Humphrey, a soft, round man with circular, wire-framed spectacles and a vast bald spot.

"On my recommendation, Lady Davenport-Witt won't be answering any questions. If you'd like to pose one, pose it to me."

"Very well," Superintendent Morris said. "It has come to the police's attention that Lady Davenport-Witt has a familial connection with the Duke of Worthington."

Felicia blurted her defence. "I only learned of that possibility yesterday." Mr. Humphrey gave her a warning look. She huffed and folded her arms across her chest in an unladylike position of defiance.

"That hardly makes her a murderer," Mr. Humphrey said.

"It gives her motive," the oafish superintendent replied. "There is a substantial inheritance on the line, much of which could've eventually gone to Miss Wright had the marriage become official."

"That isn't proof," Mr. Humphrey insisted. "You've got nothing but speculation. Besides, Lady Davenport-Witt wasn't an actual heir, which erases motive speculation."

Superintendent Morris blustered. "She might've plotted to convince the duke to include her in his will. Besides, she was in the gallery near where the shot was fired."

"Along with a handful of other people," Mr. Humphrey said. "Have you pulled all of them out?

Do you even know in absolute certainty who was up there?"

"Of course," the superintendent said, "and we've interviewed them all. Like all the other blasted folks in the church, their focus was on the bride and groom."

"I'd like to know how the police became aware that I'm related to the duke," Felicia said. "As far as I know, my grandmother was the only living person who knew this to be the truth." Felicia didn't mention that Ginger also knew, and probably Basil, if she could go by the look on his face. "She did record her life in her diary, but that was safely hidden away."

"We're investigating the source," Basil said. His boss gave him an evil eye, but Basil kept his gaze firmly on Felicia. "We were given an anonymous tip."

"Anonymous tips rarely hold up in court." Mr. Humphrey tapped the table with a short, stubby finger. "It appears that you have nothing of merit to hold my client. I recommend you release her into her husband's care. Lord Davenport-Witt is waiting in the lobby and is surely worried about his wife."

Superintendent Morris threw his meaty hands in the air. "Just don't leave London, Lady Davenport-Witt."

The superintendent lumbered out of the room as

Mr. Humphrey picked up his briefcase and stood, offering his arm to Felicia.

"Thank you, Mr. Humphrey, but if you don't mind, I'd like to speak to Chief Inspector Reed. Alone."

The lawyer's perpetually suspicious stare landed on Basil.

"It's quite all right, Mr. Humphrey," Basil said. "I'll deliver her to the earl. Please let him know his wife will be joining him shortly."

Mr. Humphrey gave a quick nod. "Very well. Good day, Lady Davenport-Witt."

He was gone before Felicia could thank him for coming to her defence, but she mused that he was merely doing his job and obligation to her beyond his contract with Charles.

Basil took the seat opposite Felicia.

"Can we be overheard?" she asked quietly. "From the listening room?"

"No," Basil said. "I've ensured that the speaker has been turned off." After a pause, he added, "What did you want to tell me?"

Felicia let out a quiet breath, wondering if she was doing the right thing, but the police had somehow learned of her private affairs.

"Is it possible that an agency beyond the police has taken an interest in this case?" Felicia asked, her mind returning to what she had once considered a ridiculous notion. She'd been *spied* on. "An interest in me in particular, and of course, the duke and Miss Wright?"

"What would make you suspect such a thing?"

"Well, for one thing, the writer of the notes knows the truth about me—and knew long before I did. And I think we can assume that neither Grandmama nor Ginger let the cat out of the bag."

Basil stared at her, the muscle in his jaw working. Felicia was sure he knew something, but why was he reticent to tell her?

"I have the right to know, Basil. I've been accused of murder, for heaven's sake. Should word get out, it could ruin my reputation. Please, I'm not the child you think I am. I've grown up these last few years."

"All right," Basil said with a note of reluctance. "I'll tell you what I know, but there are a lot of holes in my knowledge."

"Anything is better than nothing."

"Hazel Wright was Russian. Her name was Irina Kuznetsova."

Felicia felt her jaw slacken. "A Russian *spy*?" Her hypotheses weren't so far off. "Does the duke know?"

"That part isn't clear. We haven't asked him

directly yet. We're looking into her history, and nothing we've found has raised any flags."

"But why would a Russian spy want to marry him?"

"It makes sense if you think about it," Basil said. "A marriage would've secured her place in British high society. Given her financial resources and connections with powerful people."

Felicia sighed. "I suppose so. But what does all of this have to do with me?"

"Felicia, I'll speak plainly. There's no doubt in my mind that you're in danger. This killer is a good shot from long distances. You must be very careful. Stay out of sight as much as possible until he's been apprehended."

The flash in Basil's hazel eyes left no doubt in Felicia's mind that he was being sincere. "I will, Basil. I promise."

"Good." Basil got to his feet. "Now, we mustn't leave your poor husband to wait any longer."

Felicia agreed and followed Basil out of the room.

CHAPTER TWENTY-FIVE

*B*urton seemed reluctant to let Ginger into Witt House without the mistress or master at home, which Ginger thought was understandable.

"I'll only be a moment, Burton. Lady Davenport-Witt is in rather a hurry and has sent word for me to collect a few of her personal items."

"If you give me a list, I'll ask Daphne to gather them and send them by courier."

"Lady Davenport-Witt was very clear that she wanted me to go through her things. The items requested are, er, rather delicate. I do believe she's meeting up with Lord Davenport-Witt."

Ginger hoped the butler would infer that these delicate items were feminine needs for the marriage bed, and by the blush that crept up his neck, it appeared to be the case.

"Certainly, madam. Follow me."

Ginger scurried in front of the butler. The man was far too observant and caught anything amiss. "There's no need to bother," she said quickly. "I know the way."

The entrance was smaller than Hartigan House's, and the staircase was nearer to the front door. Ginger glanced over her shoulder as she headed up to ensure Burton didn't follow on her heels and was pleased to see that he had disappeared out of sight. A good butler was extremely valuable to those he served but a liability when one wanted to snoop.

Ginger passed the door to the bedroom that Felicia and Charles shared, going to the spare room Felicia used as her office. The room was decorated with a feminine flare with its floral wallpaper, plush lemon chaise longue along one wall, and in the middle of the room, a desk facing the window. A typewriter Felicia used when writing her mysteries had a sheet of paper still in the roll, where Felicia had apparently stopped writing, mid-paragraph.

As Felicia wasn't in the habit of hiding anything, trusting everyone who worked in her household as she did, Ginger quickly found what she was looking for. The photographs Felicia had taken at the wedding were in a file on her desktop. Taking a seat in Felicia's chair, Ginger used the magnifying glass she carried in her handbag to peruse each one. She didn't know what she hoped to find but mentally divided each eight-by-ten photograph into a grid, slowly moving the magnifying glass along each section. There were the shots of the altar, the carnage after the shot, and the panicked people scurrying. Many images were blurred as a result—but not the picture of the poor duke's face crumpled in grief as he took in the nightmare.

Charles was in many, as Felicia had pointed out before, and Ginger wondered what or who he suspected. He was clearly in search of something or someone.

The balcony where the few sanctioned photographers had been gathered was empty in almost all the photographs, but—Ginger held up the magnifying glass to an apparent shadow by one of the pillars. Under inspection, she could see that it wasn't a natural shadow but the form of a man. The familiarity of the image made her pause. What was *he* doing there?

As her mind pondered the strange discovery, her eyes landed on the typewriter and the page in the roll. Felicia's abandoned manuscript was left mid-paragraph with the sentence she'd been composing unfinished.

It wasn't the words that made Ginger's pulse race, but an individual letter. The misalignment became evident when she held her magnifying glass to the page. *The k left a small space behind it.*

The note writer had used Felicia's typewriter!

How had Felicia not noticed this in the notes? Perhaps her mind was so used to seeing the aberration with the *k*, it looked normal to her.

Ginger slowly registered a presence behind her and turned carefully. Keeping her cool, she said to the man whose image was captured on the balcony of St. Paul's Cathedral, "Burton? Is everything all right?"

Clearly, everything wasn't all right. The butler held a pistol, pointing it at Ginger with a steady arm. "As right as rain, madam. Now, if you'll kindly come with me."

CHAPTER TWENTY-SIX

Ginger was aware of the cellar in Witt House but hadn't had reason or opportunity to view it before now. Burton, holding a gun to her back, prodded her down from the top level of the house to the stairs behind the kitchen that led to the wine cellar, somehow evading the cook and housemaids as he did so.

The dank, musty smell common to most cellars hit Ginger's senses as she carefully manoeuvred herself down the steps, which were lit only with the dim light of Burton's torch as he followed behind. The far wall was filled with Charles' wine collection, and a few unmarked crates were stacked in the corner.

When they reached the bottom of the steps, Burton finally spoke. "There's a box of matches next to that oil lamp, Mrs. Reed. Please light it so that we can see properly."

Ginger hesitated for a moment, shooting the butler a look. He didn't even seem uncomfortable giving orders to someone of her class.

"Of course," she said. She picked up the matchbox, selected a match, and struck the head on the side of the small box, creating a flame. She inserted it into the hole at the lamp's base, lighting the wick in the oil almost as if she had invited Burton to the cellar as her guest. However, there was only one small wooden chair, and Ginger decided if one of them must remain standing, it would be the butler.

"So, now that you have me at your disposal," Ginger started, "perhaps you wouldn't mind telling me what's going on. What's happening right now?"

Though Burton kept his pistol pointed in Ginger's direction, he relaxed his stance a little, as Ginger was careful not to pose a physical threat. Burton had been careful when he led her through the house, keeping enough distance between them that Ginger didn't have an opportunity to put her self-defence skills to work to disarm the man.

"I'm afraid you're too nosy for your own good, madam."

"I've been told that before."

The butler cleared his throat. "Clearly, you're not the kind to learn from your mistakes."

"Clearly. So why don't you ease my curiosity now?"

Burton narrowed his eyes. "You know I'll have to kill you then."

"I think you're going to kill me anyway."

"Sadly, you'll be what we call in the field a civilian casualty."

"In the field?" Ginger gaped. "You're an agent?"

"Whoops! The secret's out," Burton said with a smirk.

"British government?" Ginger asked. "Or Soviet?"

"British, m'lady," he returned with derision. "It was *Miss Wright* who was the Soviet agent. She was the threat to the Crown, not me."

"Irina Kuznetsova. Is that why you killed her?"

"Ha, you are good, Mrs. Reed," Burton said with a look of admiration. "Not surprising, as you are a former agent yourself. Such a shame you've taken yourself off the agents' roster. A lady with your charm and intelligence was an asset to the service. You know, it's been under discussion what to do with you."

"What do you mean?"

"Whether you've become a liability or not. It's

why His Lordship was assigned to keep an eye on you."

Ginger exercised the skills she'd learned as an agent to keep the shock she felt from her expression, but by the look of victory in Burton's eyes, her skills needed sharpening.

"You don't think his time in Brighton, where you 'met', was an accident, did you? Or his pursuit of Miss Gold?"

Ginger felt bile rise in her throat. Felicia had expressed clear unhappiness in her marriage. Had it been a sham from the beginning?

"What part are you playing?" she asked. "Does Charles know who you are?"

"Of course he does, madam," Burton said. "We worked side by side in the war. When the war ended, it was decided that I should play the role of His *Lordship's* servant. Do you know that I saved his life? Twice? And now, he orders me around as he pleases. Even when there's no one around to witness our charade. I'm one of the country's best agents, and they've practically shelved me. Frankly, I've finished with him *and* with the service."

Ginger remained silent, hoping the quiet would stir Burton to keep talking. She didn't have long to wait before his bottled-up vitriol began to pour out.

"I've given my life in service of King and country,

and despite my stellar record, I'm consistently given pitiful assignments, like this one, whilst Charles traipses to the House of Lords every day. I'm the one who's waiting on his spoilt wife, and why should I? *I* didn't marry her?"

"Why did you write those notes to Lady Davenport-Witt?"

The corner of Burton's mouth pulled up to one side. "Just having a little fun at her expense. Do you know how boring it is to be stuck in this role as a butler? After the excitement of the war? Honestly, I thought she'd fuss over them a bit more, get Charles riled up."

Ginger couldn't stop herself from coming to Felicia's defence. "Lady Davenport-Witt is stronger than most people think. How did you know about her connection with the Duke of Worthington anyway?"

"Butlers are invisible, madam. We hear and see things. And I have special gifts for sniffing out information. And your study is unlocked." He tsked. "I admit to being slightly disappointed at how little effort you put into hiding things. I only had a few moments to flip through the old lady's diary, but it'd obviously been opened to the page of shame many times . . ." His lips pulled up. "A treasure trove of scandal, for the taking." He waved the pistol. "But that means nothing now. When I've finished here,

I'm shipping off to India where the sun shines more often than not, and I can live out the rest of my days in the lap of luxury—being waited on for a change."

Ginger didn't want to ask what he meant by "finished". The man obviously needed to say his piece.

"Eventually, it will be noticed that you are missing," Burton said. "You likely made your daft butler Digby aware you were coming here. I can't stay out of sight very long or my absence will also be noted. I'm needed upstairs to let them know you came and left, and I have no idea where you went. They'll believe me, you know."

Ginger had no doubt about that. She had had no idea of Burton's double life.

But Charles knew. No matter what Burton planned to do with her, Charles was also a liability to him and, by extension, Felicia. They were all in danger.

Ginger had left her handbag in Felicia's office, though she'd failed to carry her Remington in it, and was helpless without a weapon. She needed to keep Burton talking to buy time. "May I ask why you chose such a public event to dispose of the Soviet agent? It seems rather excessive to me."

Burton chortled. "As a challenge to myself, I suppose. Certainly, I could've furtively dispatched the spy, but what fun is there in that?"

"You did mention you were bored."

"Precisely. The thrill of deception and misdirection—I entered as a newspaper man, fake identification and whatnot. Not one person looked me in the eye. Really, anyone can crash a wedding. And if it weren't for your interference, the police and all the self-important agents, including the lord of Witt House, would be chasing their tails."

Ginger's mind had been working so hard to find a way out of this hostage situation she almost missed what Burton said next.

"I'm afraid I have to do what I brought you down here for." He cocked his pistol.

CHAPTER TWENTY-SEVEN

Felicia cast a quick side glance at Charles as he drove back to South Kensington, then steadied her gaze ahead. "Did you know?"

Charles' fingers tightened on the steering wheel. "Know what?"

"About my connection with the Worthington family. Did you know before I knew?"

Felicia's heart fell at Charles' hesitation. He *had* known? But how? And for how long? And who did he really work for? Felicia no longer believed her husband was endlessly busy with duties attached to the House of Lords.

But the most important question that bounced around in her head was, *Is he going to lie?*

Instead of answering, Charles squeezed the ball

of the brass horn and lifted a fist to a driver of a sporty roadster who hadn't been paying attention. If he thought this distraction would make her forget he hadn't answered her question, he was dead wrong.

"Charles?"

"Yes. I knew. But I didn't see how the information could improve your life."

Felicia huffed and punched Charles in the arm. "How dare you make that decision for me? I'm a grown woman. I deserve to know the truth about my life."

Charles looked appropriately chastised, his jaw twitching, but he never offered an apology.

Felicia narrowed her eyes at her husband. "What other secrets are you keeping?"

Charles stubbornly kept silent.

"How did you find out about me and the Worthingtons?" Felicia asked. "I don't know how anyone could've known that unless my grandmother revealed the truth to them herself or if they got their hands on her diary." She glared at Charles. "Is that it? Did you find the diary in Ginger's study?" If Felicia herself could find it, then Charles could've too. But why would he search Ginger's office?

All these questions and no satisfying answers were giving her a headache.

They were entering Mallowan Court when

Charles answered, "I did learn about it from Ambrosia's diary, but I didn't find it. It was shared with me."

"Ginger showed you?"

Charles parked, then turned to Felicia. "I know you're angry, and you have reason to be, but I'm asking you to trust me."

Felicia threw open the door of the motor car. "Why should I trust you, Charles, when you constantly lie to me?" She was practically jogging to the front door in her desperation to put distance between herself and Charles.

"Felicia!"

Without stopping or turning, Felicia shouted, "I don't want to talk to you right now."

Perhaps the neighbours heard her outburst, but that minor embarrassment could hardly hold a candle to the scandal about to come.

Felicia burst through the front door, surprised when Burton didn't immediately appear to take her coat. She tossed it on the coat rack, not even caring when it missed the hook and landed on the floor.

Charles, who'd quickly caught up to her, picked it up and hung it on her behalf. "I can see you're upset," he said. "Take some time to calm down, and then, perhaps, we can discuss this like adults."

Felicia spun on her heel and pointed a finger.

"Are you calling me a child? Is that how you see me? An immature bright young thing?"

"No, Felicia, of course not."

"I can reassure you that after this past year, after this, I'm no longer an ignorant girl." Felicia ran up the staircase. Pausing at the landing, she listened to ensure Charles hadn't followed her, then went to her room. Sitting at her dressing table, she took care of her face, clearing off the smudged make-up caused by obstinate tears. Her bob was a sight and she roughly brushed through to smooth it down.

What was she to do now? Confront Ginger? Why would Ginger share something so personal with Charles and not with Felicia herself? And did she really have a good reason to be so angry with him? True, he'd learned something about her and hadn't told her as he should've, but his reasons for such a decision weren't malicious. He'd honestly believed he was acting in her best interest.

And now she'd gone and made the chasm growing between them even worse. Her emotions had got the best of her, proving his point that she still acted like a child. Charles was her husband. He loved her. She loved him. They would work this out.

When Felicia left the bedroom in search of Charles, she passed the open door of her office and came to a quick stop. Something was out of place.

Backtracking, she went inside and stared at the handbag on the floor. Confused, Felicia picked it up. It wasn't one of hers. It looked like Ginger's. What was Ginger doing in her office?

Her gaze scanned her desktop. With the start of her latest mystery scrolled in the roller, the typewriter was in place, but the photographs piled beside it caught her attention. Felicia was certain those had been placed in the folder, now open and empty. And that wasn't her magnifying glass.

Felicia took a closer look. The glass was positioned over the image of a man on the balcony at St. Paul's Cathedral. Picking up the magnifying glass, Felicia adjusted the distance between it and the photograph until the face of the man became clear. She gasped. Then came the realisation of what must've happened. Ginger would never have left her handbag behind. Burton had Ginger.

Felicia started for the stairs as she shouted, "Charles! Charles!"

CHAPTER TWENTY-EIGHT

In crisis moments such as this one, time seemed to move into slow motion. Ginger had already made a mental grid map of the cellar. It would take one long step to reach the table and oil lantern. A row of wine bottles was behind her, just below shoulder level. The wooden stairs to her right, were about three paces ahead.

She could hear Burton breathing, and her heartbeat resounded in her ears. Ginger was determined not to die in Felicia's cellar. She hadn't any hope of discovery, as the cellar was the butler's domain, and none of the other staff ventured down.

She stared Burton in the eye. "Wait."

"I won't stand for stalling tactics, Mrs. Reed."

Sometimes miracles did happen. Suddenly, a faint sound of rapid footsteps overhead, as if someone was running, and then the slight creaking of the door as it opened.

"You should've oiled that," Ginger said. Taking advantage of the butler's distraction as he glanced up, she took that long step, gripped the edge of the splintery table, and pulled up hard. The table tipped with a bang, and the oil lantern crashed onto the plank floor, throwing the cellar into darkness.

"Help!" Ginger cried. Ducking behind the fallen table, she reached behind herself, gripping the neck of a wine bottle.

The light from the opening door flashed enough for Ginger to see Burton scrambling to find his gun. His fingers tightened around the grip. Ginger flung herself at the butler, landing clumsily on his back. A loud *oof* escaped his mouth. He pushed up on his hands to buck her off, and the motion nearly threw Ginger off balance. Using the momentum, she brought the wine bottle down hard on the back of Burton's head. He slumped heavily to the floor.

Ginger kicked his weapon out of reach, checked his neck for a pulse, and found it strong.

"Ginger?" Felicia came rushing down the stairs after Charles. "Are you all right?"

"Yes. Thank you for finding me."

Felicia threw her arms around Ginger. "Well, you left an obvious clue."

Charles stood over Burton.

"He's alive," Ginger said. "I got a full confession. He killed Miss Wright."

"But why?" Felicia asked. "I don't understand."

Ginger glimpsed at Charles before looking away. It wasn't her place to expose the business of the secret service.

"I'm sure the law will get to the bottom of it," Charles said, swallowing hard. "It's such a shame. He was a fine butler." He pinched his eyes shut, adding, "I thought he was a friend."

Felicia huffed. "Some friend. And I doubt *I'll* ever find out why he did what he did. I'm going upstairs to telephone the police."

When Ginger and Charles were alone, Ginger said softly. "Felicia is a strong-minded person. She won't take being put second in your life. You might lose her."

Even in the dim cellar lighting, Ginger could see Charles' ashen complexion. He sighed heavily. "I know."

LATER THAT EVENING, after the police had come and taken Burton away, Felicia sat on the settee with Charles in their sitting room. He'd poured her a drink, and then sat at the other end of the settee, turned towards her.

"I know you're upset with me," he said.

Felicia didn't see a need to deny it. "That is true."

Charles reached across the gap between them, taking her hand. "You must know that I love you."

"That's the problem, Charles. I don't know that. Not really."

"What can I do to make this right?"

"Tell me the truth!"

"I'm as honest as I can be."

Felicia considered her husband. That was probably the most honest thing he had said to her in a long time.

"I know you can't tell me everything," she finally said, "but I'm not stupid."

"I would never accuse you of anything so vile," Charles said. "You're more intelligent than I gave you credit for."

"I suppose that's a compliment," Felicia said dryly.

"That didn't come out the way I meant it. I always knew you were intelligent but also very perceptive."

"Then you'll believe me when I say I've guessed who you are, or rather *what* you are. It's taken me longer than perhaps it should've, but I think I've worked it out." At Charles' silence, she added, "I know you can't admit to it, but I know Miss Wright was a spy for the Soviet Union. And anyone with a brain knows that Britain has a roster of spies as well. With everything I know about you, let's just say, it makes sense now."

Charles' shoulders fell, deflated. "Do you want me to go away?"

"No, Charles." Felicia shifted towards him, closing the distance between them. "I want to come with you." Grabbing his face, she peered into the eyes of the man she loved. "I want to join."

Charles' breath was low and hard. "You don't know what you're asking for."

"Perhaps, but it doesn't change things. I can't bear this wall between us. I can't take another day of mindless boredom. I can't take another minute knowing you have another life I'm not part of."

Charles' chin dropped to his chest. "Oh, Felicia."

"It's that, love, or you must leave me for good." Felicia was aware of tears streaming down her face. "And if you choose that, I'll hate you forever, but I'll hate myself more."

"It's dangerous."

"I know, and I don't care. I want your life, Charles. I mean it. I want to do something worthwhile with my time on this earth and properly serve my country. I want to be at your side when I do it.

We must be a team going forward." Felicia laid down her ultimatum once again. "Or nothing at all."

Charles closed his eyes as he let out a long breath. "You could die, Felicia."

"So could you."

"If something happened to you because of this, I wouldn't be able to forgive myself."

"You'd have nothing to forgive. This is my decision. If something happens to me, it'll be my choice. My fault alone. Besides, look how long Burton had been in the service and scarcely a bruise." She grinned. "Until he went up against Ginger."

"He'll hang for what he did."

"Only because the direction to shoot Miss Wright hadn't come from the Crown."

Charles pulled her close to press his forehead against hers. "All right."

Felicia could hardly believe her ears. "All right?"

"I really don't have much of a choice. You know too much already. I've been instructed to do something about it."

Felicia pulled back, shocked. "What kind of something?"

Charles chuckled. "Not like that. I was supposed to convince you you were going mad and send you away."

"Away where?"

"I don't know. France, Greece. Do you have a relative anywhere out of Britain? It doesn't matter. I've obviously failed miserably."

"That settles it then," Felicia said, feeling triumphant. "I don't have a convenient relation on the Continent, my mind is sound, and I won't agree to a divorce." She pulled Charles close again. "You're stuck with me, and so is the Crown."

Charles chortled. "Lord help us all."

Then he kissed her. The relief Felicia felt from getting her way was followed by a heavy blanket of apprehension.

What had she just done?

CHAPTER TWENTY-NINE

*L*ater that week, Ginger played with Rosa in the upstairs nursery. Painted a pale green with plenty of white moulding, it had breezy windows looking into the back garden where one could enjoy Clement's handiwork. Rosa snatched a wooden rattle out of Ginger's hand and tried to bite into it. It had been three days since the event in the cellar at Witt House, and the euphoria that follows a break in a case and the subsequent solving of it was wearing off.

Her toddler squirmed on her lap, and Ginger broke into a song to calm her. More slowly and subdued than the Blossom Seeley performance often heard on the wireless, Ginger sang softly, "Yes sir, that's my baby, no sir, don't mean maybe . . ."

"I love it when you sing."

Ginger turned to Basil's voice and smiled. Her husband leaned against the door frame, his arms folded across his waistcoat.

"Aren't you needed at the Yard?" Ginger asked.

The police had found the rifle used to kill Miss Wright amongst Burton's items. Ballistics proved that the pistol he'd pointed at Ginger had been used to kill Mr. Farley.

Burton had "tied up loose ends" in case Mr. Farley recollected the encounter over time. Burton was in custody awaiting trial, but he'd likely hang unless the government intervened somehow. The newspapers had given a false story about a madman who'd had a grievance towards Miss Wright. Her true identity had been suppressed. Ginger understood why things would be covered up. The citizens of Britain wouldn't like knowing that foreign agents could enter the country and infiltrate the elite to find information that could be used to Britain's detriment.

Basil sauntered into the nursery. "I took the day off. I do get those on occasion." He reached his arms out to Rosa, who squealed as he lifted her into the air in a game of aeroplane. "You're Amelia Earhart!"

Ginger nodded subtly at Nanny Green, who quietly retreated to her own room, giving Ginger and Basil private family time.

"I'm so pleased that Scout is coming home tomorrow," Ginger said, longing to have her family all under one roof. "I really do miss him when he's at boarding school."

"We're giving him the best shot at life, love," Basil said as he lowered Rosa to the carpet on the floor. "He'll thank us for it."

"He's already grateful," Ginger returned in her son's defence. "I'll be happy when we get to the summer holidays."

"Time is going by fast enough, in my books," Basil said. He pointed to his temples. "Do you see this new batch of grey?"

Ginger smiled widely. "I do. And I find it rather fetching."

Basil leaned over and kissed Ginger on the top of her head. "I find *you* fetching."

Laughing, Ginger said, "Do save your wooing for later."

"Very well." Basil let out an exaggerated sigh as he took an empty chair. "If you insist. Do you have any news with which to entertain me then?"

"A letter from Haley came this morning."

"And how is your fine American friend?"

"Studying hard. She'll be a bona fide doctor soon. I really must return to Boston one day. Sally and Louisa are there." Ginger often thought about her stepmother and half-sister so far away. Louisa was an entertaining letter writer and kept Ginger in stitches with her missives about her antics and scandalous news amongst the social elite. Scandals weren't only a British thing, it turned out.

"One day," Basil offered. "And how is Felicia?"

This question seemed innocent enough, but the arrest of their butler had been a thorough shock to Felicia and Charles. Ambrosia, of course, insisted that she'd found Burton a suspicious character all along.

However, Ginger was aware that the dubious nature of the "faithful butler" only scratched the surface of what was going on at Witt House. She hoped dearly that Felicia and Charles would work things out.

"It's been difficult for her, naturally," Ginger said. "But Felicia is made of sturdy material. I know it's hard for some to believe if they've known her as a spoilt, irresponsible, bright young thing."

"Hardships have a way of tempering one," Basil said.

Ginger agreed. "One silver lining, perhaps, is the development of a new relationship between Felicia and the Duke of Worthington. The poor man is heartbroken over the loss of his love and the knowledge of her betrayal. I believe Felicia will be a salve of healing for him. And he, her, in a roundabout way."

"A happy ending after all," Basil said.

"Yes," Ginger said, stepping towards Rosa, who'd crawled off the rug. She swooped the child in her arms. "A happy ending."

Felicia was enjoying tea with the duke in the drawing room of his townhouse. They'd discussed the weather, the latest gossip in the royal family circle, and other general topics like favourite books and places to holiday.

"There's something I want to show you," the duke said. He went to a small writing desk under the window and took out a travel picture frame covered in blue morocco, a fine goatskin leather. Folding back the two wings that covered the picture, he held it out.

Felicia blinked at the painted miniature in the frame. It was like looking at her own reflection in the mirror had she been dressed like a young Queen Victoria with her hair looped over her ears and a lace cap on her head.

"That's my mother," the duke said. "Around the same age as you are now. Can you see the resemblance to yourself?"

"I can," Felicia admitted. "It's rather shocking." She placed a hand to her chest. "My heart skipped a beat. It's a lot to digest that I have an entirely different bloodline than I've believed all my life."

"I can imagine," the duke said kindly. "That painting is another reason I was quick to believe your grandmother's story about my brother."

Once onto their second cup of tea, the conversation turned to plans for the future.

"I will go back to my manor in the country. The glitz and glamour of London has lost its appeal to me now," the duke offered.

"Perhaps Charles and I will visit one day."

"Perhaps." His shoulders slumped as he glanced away.

Felicia gazed at the duke with affection. "I hope you know I'm not after an inheritance, Your Grace. And if a continued association is too painful for you, I understand."

The duke looked back. "Do you have reason to believe your grandmother would concoct such a tale?"

"I do not," Felicia said adamantly. "My grandmother may be many things, proud and stubborn among them, but she's not a liar or a deceiver. She says what she thinks and holds values like integrity and propriety dearly. It's not a matter of whether I believe her because I do. It's a matter of whether you do. And perhaps making a decision either way isn't of any consequence to you."

The duke laughed. "I most definitely see your grandmother in you—two strong ladies. And a bit of my mother as well. And I'm willing to take Lady Gold at her word. She has no reason to create such a lie at this point in her life or yours, as you've married well and finances aren't a concern. I have thought about this. I have no one else to leave things to and none left in my bloodline. I want to leave my estate to you. I only ask that when the time comes, you manage things the best you can and employ all the help you need. My estate is rather complicated."

Felicia flushed with the news. It was exactly what the superintendent had accused her of, conniving to get into the duke's good graces. "There are those who will think I orchestrated such an arrangement. Are you certain?"

"Yes. I trust you to manage my affairs with integrity. Besides, you *are* family."

"Very well, I'd be pleased to honour you that way, Your Grace."

"If you don't mind, dear, I would really like it if you would call me Uncle Percy."

Felicia smiled. "Uncle Percy."

They enjoyed cakes and scones along with another pot of tea. "I do have a bit of news, Uncle. I haven't even had a chance to tell Ginger yet, but Charles and I are going abroad for a while—to Amsterdam. To do with his work."

The work was actually Felicia's induction into the British secret service. She and Charles agreed that Ginger and Basil would become suspicious if Felicia suddenly became busy and out of touch while living in the same cul-de-sac. Charles had arranged for them to spend time in the Netherlands, where the service had a clandestine station and where Felicia would be trained.

"Amsterdam is nice this time of year," the duke said. "Will you be attending the Games of the IX Olympiad?"

"I hope so, Uncle." Ginger and Basil had mentioned going, and it would be a chance for her and Charles to see them there. "It would be a shame to be so close and miss it. Would you like to go?"

The duke, Felicia's uncle, chuckled. "I think not. I have had rather enough excitement in my life, love, but I can't wait to hear all about it from you."

The Race for Gold is Murder

The 1928 Summer Olympics in Amsterdam was a widely anticipated event bringing countries across the world together in competition. Ginger has mixed feelings about attending. She's excited that for the first time, women athletes are to be included in the competition, but with a limited number of events on offer, British female athletes declare a boycott!

When a female sprinter is found dead, it's discovered that the victim shares citizenship with two countries, England being one of them.

Was the woman killed because of her refusal to boycott, or does the murderer have more sinister motives?

Ginger and Basil find themselves assisting the Dutch police to stop the killer before another athlete fails to find the finish line.

Find it on AMAZON

FOLLOW HALEY BACK TO BOSTON
Ginger visits her friend in 1932!

DEATH ON TREMONT ROW
A Higgins & Hawke Mystery #5

Death is greatly depressing!

It's been five years since Haley Higgins she moved back from London to Boston, and in that time she'd become a doctor of pathology and the assistant pathologist at the Boston City Morgue. In her position she often assists in the solving of crimes and murders, particularly since she's been working in tandem with Samantha Hawke, an intrepid newspaper reporter and good friend.

In the spring of 1932, depression is widespread in all its forms. Haley is cheered by news that her good friend Ginger Reed, also known as Lady Gold and a former resident of Boston, is coming to visit!

Naturally, Ginger will want to spend time with her sister and stepmother, but there will certainly be time for two old friends to chum around.

Tremont Row, a bustling shopping and theatre district, is exactly the kind of place Haley and Ginger, along with Samantha, love to hang out. Until a stabbing death interferes with their shopping plans!

Haley and Samantha, continuing to fight the patriarchal barriers in their respective fields, work together to find justice for the latest victim. Is it a crime driven by the desperation of poverty, or is the motive far more sinister?

Find it on Amazon

Don't miss the next Ginger Gold mystery~

ABOUT THE AUTHOR

Lee Strauss is a USA TODAY bestselling author of The Ginger Gold Mysteries series, The Higgins & Hawke Mystery series, The Rosa Reed Mystery series (cozy historical mysteries), A Nursery Rhyme Mystery series (mystery suspense), The Light & Love series (sweet romance), The Clockwise Collection (YA time travel romance), and young adult historical fiction with over a million books read. She has titles published in German and French, and a growing audio library.

When Lee's not writing or reading she likes to cycle, hike, and stare at the ocean. She loves to drink caffè lattes and red wines in exotic places, and eat dark chocolate anywhere.

For more info on books by Lee Strauss and her social media links, visit leestraussbooks.com. To make sure you don't miss the next new release, be sure to sign up for her readers' list!

Discuss the books, ask questions, share your

opinions. Fun giveaways! Join the Lee Strauss Readers' Group on Facebook for more info.

Did you know you can follow your favourite authors on Bookbub? If you subscribe to Bookbub — (and if you don't, why don't you? - They'll send you daily emails alerting you to sales and new releases on just the kind of books you like to read!) — follow me to make sure you don't miss the next Ginger Gold Mystery!

www.leestraussbooks.com
leestraussbooks@gmail.com

Murder at Brighton Beach

Murder in Hyde Park

Murder at the Royal Albert Hall

Murder in Belgravia

Murder on Mallowan Court

Murder at the Savoy

Murder at the Circus

Murder in France

Murder at Yuletide

Murder at Madame Tussauds

Murder at St. Paul's Cathedral

Murder at the Olympics

LADY GOLD INVESTIGATES (Ginger Gold companion short stories)

Volume 1

Volume 2

Volume 3

Volume 4

Volume 5

HIGGINS & HAWKE MYSTERY SERIES (cozy 1930s historical)

The 1930s meets Rizzoli & Isles in this friendship depression era cozy mystery series.

Death at the Tavern

Death on the Tower

Death on Hanover

Death by Dancing

Death on Tremont Row

THE ROSA REED MYSTERIES

(1950s cozy historical)

Murder at High Tide

Murder on the Boardwalk

Murder at the Bomb Shelter

Murder on Location

Murder and Rock 'n Roll

Murder at the Races

Murder at the Dude Ranch

Murder in London

Murder at the Fiesta

Murder at the Weddings

A NURSERY RHYME MYSTERY SERIES(mystery/sci fi)

Marlow finds himself teamed up with intelligent and savvy Sage Farrell, a girl so far out of his league he feels blinded in her presence - literally - damned glasses! Together they work to find the identity of @gingerbreadman. Can they stop the killer before he strikes again?

Gingerbread Man

Life Is but a Dream

Hickory Dickory Dock

Twinkle Little Star

LIGHT & LOVE (sweet romance)

Set in the dazzling charm of Europe, follow Katja, Gabriella, Eva, Anna and Belle as they find strength, hope and love.

Love Song

Your Love is Sweet

In Light of Us

Lying in Starlight

PLAYING WITH MATCHES (WW2 history/romance)

A sobering but hopeful journey about how one young German boy copes with the war and propaganda. Based on true events.

A Piece of Blue String (companion short story)

THE CLOCKWISE COLLECTION (YA time travel romance)

*Casey Donovan has issues: hair, height and uncontrollable trips
to the 19th century! And now this ~ she's accidentally taken
Nate Mackenzie, the cutest boy in the school, back in time.
Awkward.*

Clockwise

Clockwiser

Like Clockwork

Counter Clockwise

Clockwork Crazy

Clocked (companion novella)

<u>Standalones</u>

Seaweed

Love, Tink